Coffee & Curves

BOOKS 0-2

L. MOONE

CONTENTS

Christmas with my Boss

CHAPTER ONE

*** Ian ***

There she is. My woman, except she doesn't know it, and probably never will.

I keep my head fixed on the papers in front of me, but the numbers are blurring and I can't for the life of me figure out what it is I'm reading. All I can focus on is her from the corner of my eye, pausing in the doorway to my office.

"Umm, Ian, do you have a minute?" she asks.

I try to be casual in the way I glance up at her, then make a show of putting the stack of papers down onto my desk.

"Yes, Emily? What can I do for you on this fine December morning?"

She smiles briefly and pushes a stray lock of her hair behind her ear.

How I wish I could have done that. Her thick, unruly curls look so inviting to the touch. So luxurious. As does the rest of her.

Emily takes a reluctant step forward, smooths down her knee-length pencil skirt, and waits for a moment.

I catch myself staring and clear my throat. "Please, take a seat."

She turns around to close the door behind her and takes a step forward. My heart jumps a few beats, before I chide myself for it. Obviously, she's not here for any of that! *Down, boy!*

"I wanted to come in…" she starts. "Shit, how do I say this?"

Now, I'm half intrigued, half terrified. Has she noticed my behaviour lately and come in to make a complaint?

The inappropriate stares towards her desk. The way in which my heart, as well as the rest of my body, seems to react to her presence. I've been playing it cool—professional—but women are more sensitive to subtle cues, aren't they?

HR will have a field day with this…

"By just telling me already," I say. Hopefully I sound confident.

"Yeah. Huh." She smiles again but avoids the sight of me. This is not going well.

"Maybe we should—Do you want some tea? I should get us a cup of tea first," she says.

Before I get the chance to say anything to stop her, she's out the door again and making a beeline for the kitchenette.

Bloody hell, I mutter under my breath as I push my chair back.

I don't know if she intended for me to follow her, but it's happening, anyway. As though my feet have a mind of their own. It could be worse. At least I don't have a hard-on. *Yet.*

The sight of her standing with her back towards me as she fills the kettle almost gives me just that, though. She's a vision of feminine perfection. Soft curves as far as the eye can see. I love that she usually wears a skirt to work. And today's wardrobe choice accentuates all of her best assets.

If only she knows how hard I've fallen… Ever since my split with Debbie, Emily has been on my mind almost constantly. Like a man obsessed, my imagination has gone wild. But I've controlled myself in her presence for the most part.

Fuck, does she know, though? Is that why she ran out of my office just now? Onto neutral territory, within earshot of all of her colleagues?

"Emily. Is something the matter?" I ask.

I watch as she lines up two clean mugs and drops in a bag of PG Tips each. We're nothing if not particular when it comes to our choice of tea in this office.

"It's just, I didn't think it would be this hard, you know?" she says.

"What is?"

She takes a deep breath and turns with her head held high this time. "I want to put in my notice.

There it is."

Then she exhales sharply and cocks her head to the side with an apologetic scowl on her face.

Weird expression aside, she's still gorgeous.

And I'm speechless for a few seconds until she nervously breaks eye contact.

"You want to—" I shake my head in shock. "Why? Are you not happy here?"

"See, this is why it's so hard. I am. It's a good job. But I think it's time for a change now." Her tone pitches toward the end of her answer, as though she's asking me, not telling me.

"Well… This comes as a surprise, that's all," I mumble.

"I'm so sorry! I know things have been tough this year." She pours the water, then adds a splash of milk, and hands me one of the mugs before picking up her own. "With the economy being what it is, and—"

"Where are you going?" I ask. *And will I see you again?*

"Actually, my friend Lauren—I've known her forever, since we were little—she's recently secured financing and is opening a boutique down in Teddington. She's a fashion designer, so she's good at all the creative stuff, but I am to help her out with the business end. Marketing, paperwork, and whatnot."

I nod and take a careful first sip of my tea. The hot liquid hits my tongue and instantly calms some of my anxiety.

Teddington… It's not very far, but not close enough to be able to accidentally run into her on my lunch break either.

"It's a good opportunity for you," I comment.

She nods.

"Well, I wish you all the best." I mean it too, sort of. She sounds excited about her plans, and I want nothing more than for her to be happy. Okay, perhaps I want *one* thing just slightly more… But that's painfully out of reach; always has been.

"Thanks, Ian!"

"I do need you to put it in writing."

"Just one more thing. I was hoping to take those holidays I've saved up this year. Lauren wants to open in early January, so there's not a lot of time to get all the work done."

My heart sinks. That means she's intending to leave even sooner than the obligatory one-month notice period. And with the way she's looking at me now, refusing her isn't even an option.

"Yeah… There's not much going on this time of year, so I don't see why not," I mumble. "I'll need your letter today, so I can file it with HR."

She leans over, puts her hand on my arm, and smiles brightly. "Of course. I'll get it done right now. Thanks so much for understanding, Ian. I was really worried about telling you."

"No problem," I say.

Fuck.

She turns and carries her own mug of tea over to her desk. There's a spring in her step that wasn't there before. Clearly, she wasn't exaggerating. Now that the news is out, she looks like a burden has been lifted off her shoulders.

Meanwhile, I can do nothing more than mindlessly rub the spot on my arm where she'd just touched me. It's as if I can still feel her fingertips pressing into me.

And that same burden she's lost has landed squarely on me.

These young girls in the office are going to be the death of me. Perhaps it's for the best that Emily is leaving before I make a complete arse out of myself.

As much as I try to convince myself of that, there's a large and very insistent part of me which disagrees. Am I really going to let her walk out of here—and out of my life—forever?

* Emily *

New year, new start.

Or, it will be, once I join Lauren's new start-up business. It's early December, and I still have another two weeks of work to get through before I make the jump, but it's all starting to feel very real now.

The thought of leaving this place behind fills me with excitement, but also a pang of sadness. I won't miss the work for sure, but the people…

I glance up from my laptop screen and toward the perpetually open door of Ian's office. By *people,* of course I meant *person.* I'm going to miss Ian.

It doesn't even make sense. He's my boss, and he's got to be around forty. I, meanwhile, am a card-carrying young millennial. With the student loans and credit card debt to prove it.

As much as midnight fantasies and early morning daydreams try to convince me otherwise, Ian would have no use for me. He'd laugh if he knew I had these inappropriate feelings for him. He's a real man, and in his eyes, I'm nothing more than a dumb kid.

That's what made it so hard to tell him I was leaving. I thought for sure I was going to blurt out something to give myself away and make these remaining two weeks even more awkward than they need to be.

I feel like a schoolgirl with a crush on a teacher. In perpetual proximity to the object of my desire, and yet infinitely far away. He'll be forever out of my reach, and so it's only appropriate that we put some distance between each other. Before I lose my mind completely.

Because there's no way a man like him could ever want a girl like me.

He's built to perfection. His chiselled jaw and salt and pepper hair are enough to get my heart beating faster. Then there are the icy blue eyes that try to pierce my soul every time he looks at me. And his body. *Oh my God.*

I know he works out, because he brings his gym bag into the office at least twice a week. And ever since his divorce last year, he's really started filling out his shirts rather nicely. Actually, that's another reason I was so grateful for Lauren's offer. Ian has always been hot, but now he's back on the market as well. And my imagination has been working overtime, conjuring up the most cliché, porny scenarios that all end the same way: with me bent over his desk.

That would never happen, obviously.

I'm not on his radar like that and it seems no one else is, either. He's been nothing but proper, even with the pretty girls in the office. And I'm not even pretty. As my mum likes to say: Perhaps I could be, if I lost a few pounds. As if I haven't tried and failed at that already!

Back to Ian. He's a real gentleman. Because with the way gossip spreads around here, an office affair would have become common knowledge immediately. As far as I know, he hasn't even been on a single date since his divorce.

So, there's no hope. And until I stop pining for what I can't have, I'll never get a *proper* boyfriend either.

I sigh and run the spell check on the letter I've just

typed up.

My resignation.

He did seem disappointed, didn't he? He must be worrying about finding a replacement for me over the holiday period. This is the worst time of year to schedule job interviews.

Unless…

No! I shake my head. *Stop it!*

I aimlessly click around the various windows open on my computer in an attempt to quiet my mind. I'm leaving. And that's final.

From the corner of my eye, I see Ian making his way to the hallway while talking on the phone. I hit 'print' on the letter and sign it, before quickly popping into his office and dumping it on the desk. Best to just leave it here, before I make things even more awkward with further conversation.

"So," Jessica rolls up beside my desk as I sit back down. "You told him?"

"Yup."

"What did he say?"

I roll my eyes. She's so nosy. "What's he supposed to say? I was supposed to put it in writing."

"Okay… Anything else?" she asks.

I shake my head. "Don't you have work to do?"

She sticks her tongue out at me and walks her office chair back to her own seat.

The fact is, I also have work to do. Instead of

risking another trip down the rabbit hole of X-rated fantasies starring Ian, I open a fresh document and start making a list.

Everything I have to finish before I leave in two weeks.

I can't help but feel even sadder now. Only two weeks to go, and I'll likely never see Ian again. I'll be leaving a part of myself behind in this office when I go.

CHAPTER TWO

* Emily *

This is it. The last few minutes of the last day at the job. Just the office Christmas party to get through, and I'm home free.

No embarrassments, no bullshit. At least none so far. *The night is still young.*

My heart is heavy. I've had a pretty good time here these past two years. Although this wasn't my first job out of college, this was the longest I've ever stuck around anywhere.

At two-to-five, I decide to escape into the hallway and call Lauren for some much-needed emotional support.

That has been my coping mechanism these past two weeks. Every time I feel like running back and telling Ian I've made a mistake and to please give me my job back, I call Lauren for a pep talk. Her enthusiasm for our upcoming joint venture is infectious.

"Hey, girl!" she answers.

"Hey…"

"You sound depressed. Last day?" Lauren asks.

"Yep."

"Did you tell him?"

I take a deep breath and roll my eyes. "Did I tell who, what?"

"Don't play dumb with me. You've only been talking about that sexy boss of yours for hours on end each time we speak," Lauren says.

"I haven't!" I exclaim.

"I talked to Ian today, and he said this, and he did that—" Lauren speaks in an artificially high pitch, just to annoy me. "Oh, during the staff meeting, Ian made this joke today… Ian, Ian, Ian!"

"Shush, woman!"

I sheepishly check both directions of the hallway. Thankfully, this particular conversation isn't being overheard. The last thing I need is for Jessica to walk past and start some last-minute gossip. I want to be able to walk out of this building with my self-respect intact.

"Well. Are you going to tell him?" Lauren asks again.

"Am I—No! Are you nuts?" Of course I'm not going to tell him.

"You'll regret it. Don't blame me if you regret it later."

"I won't." The one thing I *do* regret is telling Lauren about my crush on Ian.

"You're no help whatsoever. I'll talk to you

tomorrow."

"Okay, sweetheart. But do me a favour."

"What?" I snap.

"Tell Ian."

I hang up in a huff. Lauren means well, but I'm not fearless like her. I can't just go up to the man and—

Before I get the chance to recover, the lift doors open and Ian walks out. He nods while approaching me in the hallway. A whiff of his intoxicating cologne finds its way into my nostrils and leaves me swooning.

"Hey. You about ready?" he asks.

"Um, yeah. Sure," I say, almost choking on my own breath.

"Okay, then," he says as he starts walking again. "Better keep an eye on that cough. You don't sound too good."

I'm still trying to catch my breath as he disappears through the double doors to our office floor. *Dammit. Very smooth!*

* Ian *

Although I've played it cool these past two weeks, the ticking clock of Emily's departure has been on my mind constantly. Still, I've soldiered on until suddenly, it's Friday the 13th, and almost time to say goodbye.

Initially Emily wasn't planning to attend the annual Christmas party, but some others convinced her that it would be silly to miss out. Tonight would serve as her farewell party as well.

I'm torn. Although I'm glad I get to spend some more time near her, I'm also dreading the fact that our last few hours together are going to take place near an open bar.

As a very young company, we've had our fair share of Christmas party scandals. Hook-ups and drunken mishaps have been a regular feature during previous years, but nothing serious enough to make upper management reconsider the format of the party. It's traditionally been an opportunity for everyone to let their hair down.

Whatever drama happens at the party, tends to stay at the party. At least that's what the unofficial company motto appears to be.

Obviously I've never done anything inappropriate myself; certainly not while I was still married. As the manager, it's imperative I lead by example, but now I'm finding that my self-imposed boundaries are crumbling.

This year, I'm newly single. Mingling is definitely on my mind, but only if it's with Emily.

I still can't believe I'm having these thoughts! About an employee, no less.

Soon-to-be former employee, my mind corrects itself.

But currently an employee nonetheless. One who is at least fifteen years younger than me.

If I caught any of my mates ogle a girl her age, I'd call him a pervert. And deservedly so.

Back at my desk, I try not to think about her anymore. I close down the various spreadsheets on my laptop and take a few notes for the coming week.

It'll be the first week without Emily here. The realisation is enough to sour my mood.

I look up to find her walking back to her desk and collecting her belongings. I'll miss seeing her whenever I glance through my open door. Without catching her unmistakable sweet scent in the air, whenever I walk past her desk.

But it's for the best.

No, it's not!

Yes, it is!

I sigh and pinch the bridge of my nose. Still, inappropriate fantasies of Emily enter my mind's eye. Every time it happens, it gets harder for me to stay in control.

"Ian, can we go now?" a female voice interrupts.

I look up and find Jessica standing in the doorway. She flips her hair back and taps the watch on her wrist.

"It's past five already and I've got important work to do at the bar."

I lean back and fold my arms. "You're going to take it easy tonight? Not like last year."

"Sure, *Dad!*"

She's only teasing, of course. But her choice of words reminds me yet again why I'm supposed to let Emily go.

*** Emily ***

When I emerge from the ladies' room after changing into my outfit for the night, the rest of my colleagues are already waiting by the elevator. It's stupid and naïve, but I pulled out all the stops for tonight.

The figure-hugging black dress—although office-appropriate—is inviting stares in my direction. Or is it the red lipstick that did it? Either way, my soon-to-be former colleagues are eyeing me curiously.

The one person who isn't looking at me much at all is Ian. Efforts, wasted.

"Sorry, were you guys waiting for me?" I ask.

"Let's go already!" Jessica whines. "Nice earrings, though."

"Thanks."

We're about a dozen people in total and get the whole lift to ourselves. Normally the company would have booked a hotel for the occasion, but due to cost-cutting measures, the party has been organised in-house by another department.

Although I was hoping to position myself closer to Ian in the lift, Jessica forces her arm through mine and keeps me from moving.

"It's going to be weird without you next week,"

she says.

I nod politely. We've never been particularly close, but whatever.

"Do you have any plans for the holidays?" she chats on.

I try to answer as best I can, but Ian's non-reaction to my brand-new dress is weighing heavily on my mind.

Once we get to the correct floor, I drag Jessica along to the improvised bar immediately. A Vodka & Red Bull—Jessica's choice—takes the edge off my disappointment, barely.

We take our first sips while more of our colleagues from other departments are still pouring into the cleared-out hall. Jessica is still questioning me, this time about my new job. The moment I utter the word 'boutique', her eyes light up and a fresh barrage of questions is hurled my way. Still, I welcome the distraction.

The first two drinks go down fast. The majority of our colleagues from the rest of the company have congregated around the bar as well. Soon, we're joined by two guys I recognise by face, but not by name until now. Tom from Accounting holds on to my hand just a little too long for comfort after introducing himself.

He tries to get the conversation going, but I keep my answers as monosyllabic as I can. After the third or fourth round, loud music starts to play at the opposite end of the hall.

"Oh! They've set up a dance floor!" Jessica squeals.

I roll my eyes. "No way."

"Yes, way! Let's go!"

I shrug. Maybe now we'll finally get rid of Tom. While I follow Jessica through the crowd, I keep my eyes peeled for Ian. I don't even know why. It's not like he's interested.

Tom, meanwhile, *is* still interested. He follows us all the way past the clusters of tables which have probably been set up for dinner. *Crap*, he's going to want to dance with me.

Finally, I spot a familiar sight in the distance. Ian is sitting by himself at the furthest table overlooking the makeshift dance floor. With one hand, he's nursing a glass of whiskey on the rocks, while the other is loosening his tie.

Swoon.

Jessica tugs on my arm to get me walking again. And now that I know he's within view, I try to make it sexy too. As if I can will him to look at me if I want it desperately enough.

The alcohol is starting to have an effect as well. I'm looser, less anxious than before. Tonight is my last night here. My last chance to get Ian to pay attention to me. And if I embarrass myself, I'll never have to see any of these people again.

My reservations about dancing in front of all my colleagues have vanished as well. Who cares, they're my ex-colleagues, anyway. So, I really let myself go to the music, much to Jessica's delight.

"Yeah! You go, girl!" she cheers me on.

I take her hand and we start dancing together, rocking to the beat, swaying our hips, and letting our hair fly. *Screw it. You only live once.*

But she isn't the only one enjoying my antics. Tom has positioned himself right next to me and is trying his best to move in. I don't even care anymore, as long as he keeps his hands to himself.

He leans in, closing in on my ear with his mouth. "You're sexy, you know that."

I try to ignore him and step in the opposite direction, closer to Jessica. I'm trying to be, but not for him. I feel eyes on me from behind, and I hope beyond hope I've finally got Ian's attention too.

The song changes to something slower, and Tom puts his hand on my shoulder. "Wanna dance with me?"

"What?" I shake my head and smile blankly.

"Dance with me, Emily. Stop being a tease!"

I grab Jessica instead, who starts giggling uncontrollably. *God*, she's such a lightweight.

Halfway through the song, she loses interest in me, though, because the other guy from the bar has turned up. She pairs up with him, and I'm stuck next to Tom, who's holding out his arms expectantly in my direction.

Oh hell, no.

I steal a glance across the room and see Ian is still sitting in the same place. His drink is now empty, but he's still holding the glass mid-air.

Is he looking at me? Maybe it wouldn't be so bad to have one little dance with Tom. In case it makes Ian realise what he's missing out on…

So, I capitulate, and Tom eagerly places his hands on my hips and we start to sway in unison for the remainder of the slow ballad that's playing. Once the music stops, I'm keen to get away from him again, but he won't let me go so easily.

I push at his arms, but they remain firmly in place on my waist.

"Come on now, let me go," I complain.

He has his head cocked to one side and is staring at my lips.

"How come we never talked before, huh? Working in the same building and all," he says. His words are slurring ever so slightly.

I pull a face and shake my head. "It's my last day today."

"All the more reason, baby."

I frown and look across at Jessica, who's already face-sucking her guy.

"See, they've got the right idea," Tom says. "Just one taste of those plump lips of yours."

Yuck! The mere idea of Tom's sloppy drunken kisses gives me the creeps. So, I try again to pry his hands off me. He dives in and I lean back as far as possible, bracing myself for the inevitable.

But it never happens. His lips never touch mine, and his fingers stop digging into me as well.

"That's enough of that!" a male voice growls.

My eyes snap open to catch a glimpse of Ian, grabbing Tom by the shoulder and dragging him backwards.

Am I dreaming? Did I pass out?

Tom's face is red with embarrassment. "Mind your own business, old man!"

Ian tightens his grip on Tom's collar and shoves him back again. He's a good few inches taller than Tom, and obviously those regular gym sessions have paid off as well.

He takes my breath away.

"Back off or don't even think about coming in on Monday morning," Ian threatens.

That particular threat had the desired effect and Tom stumbles away.

I find myself off-kilter and utterly shocked. My knees try to buckle underneath me, but Ian is right there and steadies me with both hands against my bare arms.

I look up into his steely blue eyes and lose myself in a fantasy I've had countless times before.

24

CHAPTER THREE

*** Ian ***

I shouldn't have gotten involved. But the circumstances really didn't give me much of a choice.

"Uhh, thanks," Emily says, while looking up at me with those big green eyes of hers.

Ever since she reappeared from the bathroom after her costume change, I didn't know where to look. She's a beauty no matter what she wears, but that dress… And those heels!

I nearly forgot all my previous reservations seeing her all dolled up. That's when I realised I couldn't afford to pay her too much attention. As much as I tried, I couldn't ignore her either.

Neither could anyone else, it seemed. Unfortunately for the idiot kid who works in the Accounts department, he unwittingly got in the way of my protective instinct. A powerful force of nature that *she* awoke in me.

Emily shouldn't have followed Jessica to the bar and slammed down those drinks. That was stupid; it made her look like an easy target. But then, she's still young and obviously wanted to have a good time tonight. Her last night before leaving.

I can't fault her for that, can I?

"You're okay?" I ask under my breath.

As hard as I try to hold my breath, her seductive perfume makes its way into my lungs, anyway. Our bodies are so close, it's setting my entire being alight. Her chest rises and falls rapidly with each breath, inviting me to glance downward more than once.

She's gorgeous. Curves in all the right places. But I already knew that.

The music intensifies and everyone starts dancing again. I lead her away from the crowd.

She never once looks away from me, and the last of my defences crumble to dust.

"We're under the mistletoe," she whispers, nodding upwards.

She's right, though I never even planned for that. It's a sad-looking thing, hung by a jute string and taped to the false ceiling overhead.

I look down again, mesmerised by her red painted lips, slightly parted as they are, inviting me in.

"You have no idea how hard I'm trying not to do something about that," I say.

If she's really hearing me, she's not letting on. The innocence in her eyes never wanes. Maybe I never said it out loud.

"Do it then," she mouths. So she did hear.

I can't stand it any longer and move in for that

much awaited first taste of her lips. The world around us had already vanished for me, but now even the last doubts are wiped from my mind. This is right. This is just.

I must have her. I *am* having her.

And I'll never let her go after this.

Her lips part further, and I find that her tongue is already waiting for me. I slip my arms around her and bring her in closer. Her body yields with ease. There's none of the fight I saw earlier with that kid, Tom. No hesitation, no protest.

She readily gives herself to me. Lips to lips, tongue to tongue. Our first kiss crushes my doubts and reservations to a pulp.

Her fingers twitch on my shoulders, digging into the smooth fabric of my suit. Meanwhile, my hands go on a journey of their own, exploring the curvature of her back.

How soft she feels. Absolute feminine perfection. I'm hot and cold all at the same time. My heart is racing like never before.

Even in my wildest dreams I never expected to feel this level of exhilaration.

Our kisses started gentle, tentative, but now they've intensified. We're both hungry for what the other has to give. She presses her body against me and my mind goes blank. How I wish for her hands on me. Those elegant fingers gripping my cock, which is already aching for her.

Intellect and rationalisations make way for base instinct. I want nothing more than to take things further. To possess her entire body in the same way. To let my mouth roam her luxurious curves and give her pleasure like she's never known before.

I'm hard as a rock for her, as I've been many times before. But I always denied myself the satisfaction of following through on these urges. It felt wrong, dirty. But is it, really? We're both consenting adults, right?

This isn't the time or place, though. We're at the company Christmas party, for fuck's sake. The whole staff including upper management is here, observing our little moment.

Suddenly overcome with guilt, I pull away from Emily. The spell is broken.

I think I see the sting of loss in her eyes. Or perhaps my own feelings are colouring my perception. The last thing I want is for this moment to end. Even if it's the right thing to do.

I let go of her and avert my gaze.

"Excuse me for a moment, will you, Ian?" she stammers.

I swallow hard and nod. What else can I do?

Only when she walks away, balancing unsteadily on those sky-high heels of hers, does the red fog of passion lift entirely. In its wake, shame overwhelms me. *Shit.*

Now I've done it.

She already had one creep after her who wasn't taking 'no' for an answer, and then I took it several steps further, crossing the ironclad boundary that should exist between manager and employee. I put my hands on her *and* kissed her! I should be ashamed of myself.

A glance around the room reveals that most of the crowd are too preoccupied in their own celebrations to notice my indiscretion. None of the company's VPs are within view either. *Thank God for that at least.*

But it is very clear to me that the time has come to leave this event behind. Emily has made her escape, no doubt to get away from me, and now it's my turn. Clearly I can't be trusted around her. Not now, not ever.

I'll have to make things right with her somehow, apologise for my outrageous behaviour. Just how I will do that without losing it again, I don't know.

I make my way through the same crowds Emily had negotiated earlier, until I'm accosted by Jessica.

"Where you off to, boss?"

I mumble something dismissive and leave her standing there.

* Emily *

What the hell just happened?

As I find myself staring in the mirror of the ladies' room for the second time, a mere hour after getting ready for this party, I can't believe what just went down. Ian wasn't interested in me; he couldn't be!

So why did he come to my rescue with Tom? He was just being a good boss, right? Taking care of me before things escalated into something that HR would have to get involved in.

But did we actually just kiss immediately afterwards?

"No flipping way," I mumble under my breath.

I lean closer to the mirror and clean up my smudged lipstick.

It's because I dared him, isn't it? I pointed out that we were standing under the mistletoe, so he had to act on it. It's tradition after all.

It didn't *mean* anything, did it? It was all in good fun.

My mind is racing toward a million potential outcomes. But the numerous cocktails I've downed are clouding my brain.

All I know is how I feel. Ian's strong hands turned me to jelly. His lips on mine knocked the wind out of me. And as soon as he let go, my fight or flight instinct kicked into high gear.

I've never been a fighter, so I ran in here.

Something I regret now; I should have faced him to figure out his intent.

And what's worse, I can't seem to muster the courage to go back out there. What am I going to say to Ian? We were just getting caught up in the moment, but now the feeling is gone.

If he figures out just how much I've wanted him this past year, he'll think I'm pathetic. All the liquid courage I'd built up is dissipating. I open my clutch purse with trembling fingers and retrieve my phone.

"Lauren," I cry out.

"You told him?"

I take a deep breath and give her the full account, in minute detail. Everything that happened with Tom, Ian's intervention, and our resulting kiss.

"Are you still there?" I ask at last.

"Yeah, I'm still here. Em. You've got to go to him."

"But…"

"Listen to me carefully. You have got to go back out there and tell him *everything*," she says.

"He'll think I'm a total loser. We were under the mistletoe and that's why—" I close my eyes and think back to the exact moment he kissed me. My knees are weak all over again.

"This is good news, Em! He's into you too. Or nothing would have never happened."

"But…" I protest.

"Did he or did he not almost punch out some guy just because he was creeping on you?"

"I wouldn't put it quite like—" I stammer.

"He did. Because he likes you." Lauren sounds triumphant. Or smug. Or both.

"Bullshit!" I say.

"Emily and Ian, sitting in a tree…"

That's enough to make me hang up on her again, for the second time tonight. With friends like these…

Lauren is right about one thing, though. I can't spend the rest of the evening hiding in the ladies' room. And I could use another drink to stave off the shame and regret.

I hate being such a coward when it comes to men.

And so, I take one last deep breath, fix my hair, and make my way outside. Unfortunately, the hallway isn't as empty as it was earlier. Tom is hanging around right outside.

But I'm determined not to let him intimidate me. Not this time. I pass him with my head held high.

"You didn't have to be such a bitch about it," he mumbles.

"What?" I don't know why, but his remark enrages me and I turn on my heel to square off against him.

"Leading me on when you've got a boyfriend already. It was a bitch move."

"The fuck?" I put my hands on my hips and stare him down. "I wasn't leading you on. Just because I let you dance with me for a minute doesn't give you the right—"

"You know what, I'm over it. Have a nice life with what's-his-name!" Tom turns away and hits the lift button three or four times in quick succession.

"Maybe I will!" I shout, while stomping back through the double doors leading to the party.

"Good!" he calls after me.

What an asshole! Now I wish Ian *had* punched Tom. He would have deserved it.

Once inside, I scan the room but I don't see Ian anywhere. There are plenty of classy suits within view, but he isn't one of them. So instead, I head for the bar, where I run into Jessica.

It's not even seven o'clock yet, and she's a mess.

"Girl! Where you been?" she slurs.

"Bathroom." I continue to look for Ian in the crowd, to no avail.

"Looking for Ian?" she asks.

I give her a probing look. Considering how sloshed she appears; she's still got better observational skills than anyone I know. Except maybe Lauren.

"What if I am?"

"He's gone up. Work."

"Ah." *That's not a good sign, is it?*

She winks at me and wanders off, back toward the dance floor, leaving me with a tangle of thoughts in my head. I try not to let all my insecurities drag me down, but they're bubbling up to the surface again.

Clearly, he's embarrassed by what happened, that's why he left the party already. He regrets it.

A man like Ian could never be into you!

Or… is he hoping I'll follow him up? Nah, that's impossible!

The simplest answer is probably the right one, I remind myself.

I tried very hard to impress him tonight. This dress and the over the top make-up even earned me a kiss under the mistletoe, but I'm still *me*. An ordinary looking twenty-four-year-old with a bit too much padding around the waist, as well as everywhere else.

Whereas Ian is… Perfect. Movie star perfect, even. The leading men of Hollywood have nothing on him.

I might as well leave too. Our kiss was the highlight of the evening. The highlight of my year, perhaps even my life so far.

Lauren's words still ring in my ears. *He's into you. Or nothing would have happened.*

I bite my bottom lip and try to ignore the heaviness in my chest. At the off chance that she's onto something, am I willing to leave things like this, without even trying to talk to him? I may never see him again after tonight.

Ugh, I hate this. I hate having to put myself out there!

Still, I know I have no other choice. Rather than turn up in his office empty-handed, I head to the bar and get a couple of drinks. Scotch on the rocks, like what I saw him drinking earlier.

By the time I reach the lift, my heart is all the way up in my throat. Undeterred, I make my way up to what used to be my workplace until an hour or so ago.

The entire floor is dim, except for the lit-up doorway at the end. Ian's office.

I take a deep breath, and another, while trying to overcome the inertia in my legs.

"Ian," I call out. "Can we talk?"

CHAPTER FOUR

*** Ian ***

What do they say about the best-laid plans? Doomed to fail.

That's exactly what's happening.

I had left the party and retreated to my office with one clear aim: to stay as far away from Emily as possible. Because after months of keeping my desire for her under wraps, I simply couldn't take it anymore. Not with the countdown of her departure hanging over our heads.

Our kiss downstairs had proved very clearly that I couldn't trust myself around her. I had gone too far.

"Ian, can we talk?" her voice echoes against the empty floor outside.

I close my eyes and take a deep breath. She's here for an apology. I can't deal with this right now. I ought to tell her I'm waiting for an important call, or just ignore her in the hopes that she'll go away, or...

"Sure, come on in," I hear myself say instead.

There she is, a vision of beauty, pausing in the doorway to my office. Her eyes aimlessly dart around the room, never fixating on me for more than a split second.

It's a good thing I'm sitting down, because my body is still reeling with the effects our kiss has had on me. My cock is straining painfully against my zip. This sort of thing hasn't happened publicly since I was a teenager. My fingers are itching to take care of it right now, underneath my desk, with her still in the room.

That is sexual harassment, I try to convince myself. *Keep it in your fucking pants!*

"I…" we both start talking at the same time.

"No, sorry, you go ahead," I say.

"I know you wouldn't have meant anything by it," she says.

"Right," I say, although that couldn't have been further from the truth. It meant *everything.*

"But I wanted to say thanks for handling Tom."

"You're welcome." My responses are almost robotic, as if I'm running on autopilot while the blood flow from my brain has diverted down south.

"Well, anyway, I got you a refill," she adds, while placing one of the glasses down on my desk and sliding it towards me. "Cheers?"

I raise the glass in her direction, and she follows my example. "Cheers."

Her plump red lips touch the glass to take a sip, and I can't stop staring. I know what they feel like now. What she tastes like.

"You shouldn't have come here," I mutter.

"Hm?" she looks up again. Innocent green eyes, as if she has no clue what she's doing to me. To be fair, she probably doesn't.

"I think it'll be best if you leave right now, or—"

"Or?" Her eyes challenge me briefly, before she looks away.

Have mercy! How much more of this am I meant to take?

I empty my glass in one gulp and slam it down onto the desk. The amber liquid burns slightly as it fills my throat. This isn't the good stuff, but I already knew that after sampling it earlier. The loud noise makes her flinch, but she doesn't heed my warning and stays frozen in place.

Before I know it, I'm on my feet and moving in on her position.

She's vulnerable to me. Defenceless. And I'm about to go too far again.

"This is inappropriate," I remark.

"Whatever happens at the Christmas party…" she whispers.

That's it; I'm a goner. I cup her face with both hands and guide her lips against mine again.

Her floral scent overwhelms me, but this time I don't even try to fight it.

Why don't you stop me? Why didn't you run?

She returns my kisses with even more urgency

than she did downstairs. Could it be that she's actually into it as much as I am? It doesn't seem likely, and yet…

Her hands slip underneath my suit jacket and rest on my chest. I wish I could feel her touch against my bare skin instead.

She moans into my mouth when I let my right hand slip down her back and rest it firmly on her ass. I grind into her, overcome by lust when my trapped boner rubs past the gentle curve of her stomach. God, she's sexy.

She's everything I could ever want. A goddess among women.

Heaven on earth.

"Someone stop me," I mumble.

"No way."

I swing her around and clear the desk with one smooth motion of my arm. Both our glasses shatter on the floor. It doesn't matter. Nothing does, except the fantasy playing out in front of me.

I guide her backwards until her thick buttocks press up against the edge of my desk. I lay her down gently, with as much care as I can muster in this impaired condition.

She yields easily when I force the bottom of her fitted dress up over her thighs. Creamy white skin, covered only in the thinnest sheer stockings. I peel the pretty black lace panty down and over her hips and am awestruck by the beauty of her perfect little pussy.

My cock is begging to be released, to claim her body as his own. But I know what I must do first. I will earn her approval before even thinking about my own release. I lick my lips in anticipation.

"You're gorgeous," I growl. "Let me taste you."

*** Emily ***

I'm in heaven. With one hand in Ian's hair, and the other white-knuckling the edge of the desk to keep me in place, there's not much else I can do except enjoy the ride.

He dives between my thighs and kisses my *other lips*, sending me into a fit of ecstasy. I never even considered it, but this is exactly what I need.

At this rate, the moment won't last. I'm too far gone. Too close to salvation.

My breaths are shallow and urgent. Any more of this and my chest might just explode.

But he's only just begun. Determined and confident, like only an experienced man could be, he's giving me everything I need and more.

His tongue teases me, his hot breath tickles. Although the air stings cold against the bare skin of my lower torso, I'm hotter than I've ever been.

This right here is the culmination of a million illicit dreams. I've only been pining for him for years; ever since I first set foot in this office, in fact. But I never thought this could actually happen. Initially, of course, he was married. But even after that, it didn't seem possible that he would want me that way too. He never showed any interest. Not for me, nor for anyone else at the office.

Whether this right here is happening by coincidence or convenience, I really don't care. I'm determined to enjoy our encounter for as long as it lasts.

"Oh yeah," I moan. "Right there."

The way he flicks his tongue across my clit has me panting for air. He knows exactly what he's doing. Light teases make way for firmer licks.

I lift my head to take in the view. His hands tighten on my thighs as he enters me with his tongue for the first time. I buck my hips upwards to meet his mouth. As good as it feels, there's an itch deep inside of me which is still not getting scratched.

The look in his eyes is something I've never seen before. Professional and business-like Ian has left the building. The man between my legs is wild and untamed. I'm determined to see just how much further he can be pushed.

We'll go all the way, I try to promise myself. *I'm not leaving his office before I live out that ultimate dream.*

His pale blue eyes are on me as he continues to lick and tongue-fuck me. In and out, faster and harder now. He knows just what to do.

I've had boyfriends—been with men before. But never have I experienced anything as intense as this. None of them were particularly talented in the bedroom department. I didn't think I could hook a stud, anyway. Those always go for the skinny, pretty girls, don't they?

My stomach is clenching and tears are stinging in the corners of my eyes.

Right now, I couldn't get up if I wanted to. My knees wouldn't be able to hold my weight. All I can do is lie back down on his desk and surrender to the beauty of the moment.

When his lips close around my clit one final time, I'm done for. My body tenses, and my back arches up high. Pleasure courses through my veins, making me cry out his name.

"Oh God, Ian!"

I only barely manage to stop myself before my thighs crush down on his head.

He withdraws and slips two fingers into my dripping cunt. That only makes me scream louder.

Ian leans over me and kisses my mouth again. Deeply, forcefully, he silences my cries.

My orgasm washes over me like a crashing wave, before slowly retreating again.

He tastes of me, but I don't mind. Knowing that those are *my* juices sticking to his handsome face makes me feel powerful like I never have before.

Of all the men I've ever dreamt about, nobody has ever made me feel like this. Even my wildest fantasies couldn't compare.

Endless seconds pass before I'm able to utter a coherent word.

"That was amazing," I whisper against his mouth.

CHAPTER FIVE

*** Ian ***

Although I'm still aching for my own release, the sight of a breathless post-orgasmic Emily lying on my desk fills me with a deep sense of satisfaction. I've outdone myself. Although her lipstick is smudged and her mascara has started to run a little, she's still beautiful. She doesn't need the make-up, the clothes, the high heels, or fancy perfume. Everything about her is perfect as it is.

I can't get enough of her sweet lips; kissing and nibbling at them, tasting her tongue, all while enjoying her touch on my shoulders and chest. To know that she's into it all; that she's at least somewhat attracted to me too is a wondrous thing.

"That was amazing," she whispers, almost too faint to hear properly.

I grin and kiss her harder again. "Just you wait for what's to come."

Her hand travels down my chest and abs, reluctantly at first. But when she finds the rock-solid bulge in my trousers, she starts to touch me more confidently.

I can hardly think anymore, so desperate am I for more of her affections.

"See what you do to me," I growl. It's all for her. For as long as she'll have me.

She starts to undo my belt, then struggles furiously with the buttons on the waistband. Meanwhile I allow my own hands a freer rein over her body.

Those luscious breasts I haven't dared to touch so far…

She's a real woman alright. All natural and with a body to die for. Wherever I touch her, her flesh accommodates my fingers with ease. Silky smooth, seductive as well as luxurious.

"Ohh," she moans as I squeeze her breast more firmly. It's more than a handful. Quite a bit more.

Our game intensifies. Her own hands start moving again, and finally I'm released from the confines of my suit trousers. She slides my boxer briefs down and my erection springs forwards against her upper thigh.

"You're huge," she whispers.

"It's all for you. Always will be." These words slip out before I can stop myself. But I don't get the chance to backtrack.

My mind goes blank when her fingers close around my shaft for the first time. I'm already painfully close. The only thing stopping me from exploding all over her perfect body is sheer willpower. This load is for her, yes, but I'm determined to deposit it deep within that sweet pussy of hers.

Somewhere through the fog cluttering my mind, I hear her speak a solitary word. "Why?"

I open my eyes again and find her already staring up at me. I try to answer her with another kiss.

"Why me?" she repeats.

I don't understand the question. She's the most beautiful woman I've ever laid eyes on. On a scale of 1 to 10, she's a 20.

"I could ask you the same thing," I respond.

She pumps my cock again, as if to make a point I have yet to understand. Whatever it is, I need more of the same. More of everything she's willing to give me.

Dissatisfied with the remaining barriers between us, I start unbuttoning my shirt and cast it off. Then, I back away from her just far enough to flip her onto her stomach.

I unzip her dress all the way down and am greeted by a vast expanse of perfect skin. Just as I'd hoped. She's a work of art, just waiting to be painted or sculpted. If there is a God, he created the miracle that is Emily personally, without interference from anyone else.

She turns over and leans up against her right hand. The unzipped dress is still draped over her perfect body as she stares at me through thick lashes. Top to bottom, she scrutinises my naked form.

I can only hope that she finds me worthy.

Her left hand protectively tightens around her torso. As though she isn't ready to let the dress go just yet. "Can you get the light?" she asks.

I frown. And miss out on the glorious view?

"Please?" she begs.

I really don't want to, but I can't refuse her request. The tables are turned. I'm not her boss anymore, but she is mine. She owns me now. I would move heaven and hell to keep her happy.

"Your wish is my command," I say, while stepping back towards the light switch by the door.

Even with the ceiling lamp off, there is enough ambient light coming in from the emergency exit signs on the office floor. I've still got some of my view, diffused as it is.

I offer her my hand and she gets up in front of me. The dress falls off her shoulders, down her broad hips, and onto the floor. I inhale sharply. Her floral scent fills my lungs. I'll never get enough of her natural perfume. It's as if she was made just for me. Every little thing about her drives me wild.

"You're beautiful," I say, as I cup her face again and kiss her lips.

Like a starved man, I keep coming back for more. Another taste of her, and another.

The salty sweetness of her pussy still lingers on my tongue. I wonder if she can taste herself on me.

Never have I felt this way. This deep, dark urge to

chase every depravity known to man… It's new to me. She brings up the best and worst in me all at once.

Now, she reaches for my cock again, handling it more firmly, and sending me ever closer to the edge of control. I have to do something and quick, or I'll lose it.

* Emily *

I still can't believe what is happening.

The desperation I'd felt just an hour ago when I wasn't sure what he wanted. The utter confusion he left in his wake after our first kiss.

His large hands find their way back to my breasts, caressing and fondling. He takes my nipples in between his fingers and tweaks them ever so gently.

Electric shocks pass through me; intense, but not at all unpleasant.

Then, just as suddenly, I'm thrust into another illicit dream of mine. He flips me around again and starts stroking my generous ass.

"God, I want you so badly," he growls behind me, while bringing the palm of his hand down against one of my cheeks. The sting against my skin gives me courage I've never known before.

"What are you waiting for, then?" I challenge him.

Our exchange is straight from a sleazy porno, and yet it feels completely genuine.

We aren't just actors playing a part; reading out a badly written script. I need for him to take me, just as I'd fantasised about so many times before.

I lean down over his desk and present myself to him. Although I made him turn off the lights, it's really not very dark in here. Until a moment ago, I was still nervous about how he'd react once my dress came off. I should have known better.

He isn't blind. Anyone with half a brain would know that I'm equally big with my clothes off as I am with them on. No matter how good the cut of my dress is. Or how hard I tried to suck in my stomach all evening.

My body doesn't come as a surprise to him; at least not a bad one. I'm on display in front of an appreciative, even enthusiastic audience of one.

He's taking his time, caressing me, lavishing attention on every last part of me. With his fingertips, even his lips, as he leans down after me, and plants hot kisses down my spine.

I try to turn around, to get another good look at him. My Adonis with the perfect abs. But he won't let me. A large, strong hand on my back pushes me back down.

The icy cold surface of the desk takes my breath away. But it's Ian to the rescue, with his hot cock, knocking right at my entrance.

I hold my breath and shuffle backwards as much

as I can to meet him. His fingers dig into my hip and he pushes into me, hard.

"Oh, fuck!" I cry out.

He's big. Huge, even. His dick stretches me to my limits and smothers the last of my lingering insecurities. It's more effective than any therapy or breathing exercise could be.

Although I've already cum once today, I know I have more to give, and he seems intent on taking it from me.

My feet struggle for grip on the floor, but it doesn't matter. His hands, strategically placed at my hip and back of my neck, keep me firmly pinned in place. His movements are smooth and deliberate as he plunges into me.

I've never felt this way. Powerful, coveted, and a little dirty.

He speeds up, little by little, thrusting into me again and again until I can feel his movements change. He's lost in the moment, as am I. Gone is the control he'd shown only minutes ago. He's gearing up for the grand finale.

"Please, Emily, can I cum in you?" he asks through gritted teeth.

I close my eyes and cry out. "Please, yes!"

Just as he starts to slam into me harder, burying his cock into me as deeply as it will go with each push, I'm lost for words again. My lower abdomen tightens, making me moan uncontrollably. Salvation is so close; I can taste it.

He digs his fingers into the soft flesh covering my hips and shudders to a halt. Then it happens. His dick squirms, shooting a hot load of semen right into my depths. That's all I needed to push me over the edge again.

"Fuck!" I scream, grinding back against his hips in an attempt to make the moment last.

CHAPTER SIX

* Ian *

We're both panting for air. Limp, sweaty, spent.

I look down at her naked form draped across my desk. She's truly something.

Although I would have wanted to last longer, it was an impossibility. I had a hard time controlling myself around her with her clothes on. With her naked, there was no hope in hell to stretch this out any longer.

I pull out of her and gather her up in my arms. She looks up at me. Even with the lights out, her eyes seem to shine and sparkle like expertly cut emeralds.

She opens her mouth, but I don't wait to hear what she has to say before planting my lips against hers.

Her hands are back on me, resting against my bare chest, while I tighten my grip on her. It's a beautiful moment, fleeting as it is. I hope she understands my intentions. That I want to see her satisfied. Happy.

If she'll have me, I'll spend the rest of my life doing just that. Giving her everything her heart desires.

But as our kisses lose their intensity, her hands on me become restless. I pull back and look down at her expressive eyes again.

"Ian, I had no idea," she whispers.

"Me neither."

She smiles momentarily, then glances past me at the dimly lit workstations outside my office.

"It was my last day today. When I walk out of here tonight, I'm never coming back," she remarks.

Her words sting me deeply, but I try not to let it show. She has no idea that during those dark mornings after Debbie and I split and I didn't feel like coming into work, she was the one who brought me in, anyway. There are a lot of things I've done these last few months which I probably wouldn't have bothered with if it wasn't for her.

"A new beginning," I respond.

She nods. "I hope it's a good one."

There's a finality in her words as well as her tone that makes me retreat again. Perhaps this was all that was in store for us. Our moment—perfect as it was—has passed.

I try not to dwell on it, but how can I not? For a precious thirty minutes or so, I had everything I wanted in this world. We've made memories I'll carry with me forever, even if they'll bring me nothing but heartache once she's gone.

For sure I thought that I felt a connection. That

she felt our attraction equally deeply; that there was hope for something beyond just one night. But it seems that I was mistaken.

It was all wishful thinking on my part.

I want nothing more than to pull her into my arms again and tell her that she's the one for me. But it almost seems silly now, after she's made it clear that she still intends to walk out of my life tonight.

If I'm going to convince her otherwise, a rushed confession isn't going to do it. Maybe I'll propose a dinner date. An excuse to see her again sometime.

* Emily *

"Are you hungry?" Ian asks, while brushing a damp lock of hair out of my face.

I smile briefly. No, not really, but I don't want to seem difficult or childish. If I could just feel his arms around me again, my hunger would be sated.

But I don't tell him that. Instead, I shrug and mumble: "Sure. I could eat."

What was this? A hook-up, or something more? *He's just being a proper gentleman,* I try to tell myself.

"They've probably opened the buffet," he remarks, while picking up my dress from the floor and handing it to me. "Here, you must be cold."

I wasn't, not yet, but his warm hand briefly caressing my bare shoulder sends shivers down my spine.

Just now, it hit me again that this is the end. That after tonight, I wouldn't be coming into this office anymore. I let those painful words slip out because I was hoping for him to intervene somehow. To tell me that it didn't need to mean goodbye.

He said nothing of the sort. And I feel like an idiot for ever getting my hopes up.

I close my eyes just to get a handle on myself. It's pointless, because his sheer presence makes me feel weak. Just how I'll manage on my own after this, I don't know. We shared this evening; this perfect moment, but that's all. Before long, it'll be time to face the end.

What happens at the Christmas party, stays at the Christmas party...

Because surely, that's all this is. An ill-advised fling after one too many drinks.

My eyes start to sting with the onset of tears, but I take a deep breath and force them back down. Way to ruin perfectly good sex with the man of my dreams. By breaking down and making a fool of myself. I owe it to myself to walk out of here with my head held high.

I balance unsteadily on one leg, and then the other, to step into my dress. As excited as I'd felt when it finally came off, now I'm just deflated.

"Zip me up?" I say.

He does as I ask, without uttering another word.

When his finger brushes against the back of my neck, I hold my breath and stay completely still. All I want is more of the same. Another kiss. Another caress.

My heart is still racing after that second orgasm. I'm still floaty and a little high. But reality has sunk in hard and sucked the joy out of me.

Just like before, after that first confusing kiss under the mistletoe, I feel like running away again. But this time there's no one to call for support. No plan to hatch and nothing to do, except mourn my loss.

Ian is everything I dreamed of and more, but he obviously isn't into me that much.

"I'll go down first, you follow later, so people don't get suspicious," I tell him.

He nods in agreement.

I don't know how I manage, but I do walk out of his office with my self-worth still intact. It's all an act, because on the inside my heart has already shattered. The confident stance, the purposeful strides that carry me across the abandoned office and toward the lift… I'm putting on a show, not just for him but for myself as well.

As hard as I try, I can't maintain the act. The second I step inside the elevator, I break down and let the tears flow freely.

I have no intention of going back to the party for dinner. Not in the state I'm in now. So, I press the button for the ground floor instead.

A quick search of my purse reveals that I've run out of tissues, so I can't even clean myself up, confirming the need for me to make a clean exit.

Then, it occurs to me that I don't have my coat either. I left it at my desk earlier, thinking I'll grab it after the party.

"I'm such an idiot!" I complain to myself while stabbing the button multiple times to head back up. With a bit of luck, Ian will still be getting dressed. And if not, I'll hide out in the bathroom until he leaves.

I shuffle restlessly from one leg to the other and watch the overhead display until it stops at the right floor.

"Please, please, please," I whisper. *Let me grab my coat and slip away unseen!*

* Ian *

I'm still buttoning up my shirt as I watch her disappear through the two double doors at the end of the office.

My chest tightens and my heart rate speeds up again. Something feels off about this situation, but I can't quite put my finger on what it is.

In the two years I've admired Emily from afar, I'd like to think I learnt a couple of things about her. She doesn't handle confrontation well. Her hesitation two weeks ago while giving notice was a prime example. Rather than face an issue head-on, she has a tendency to—

When the realisation hits me, my heart sinks even further.

Her remark earlier, that was goodbye. She has no intention of sticking around after this!

My heart skips a beat, and although I'm not even properly dressed yet, I find myself chasing her earlier route to the lift.

I should have said something to her right then and there. Rather than try to play it cool like I usually do, I should have told her how I *really* feel. I should have asked her out, made it clear that I want more than just a quickie in my office. And now, if I don't hurry, it'll be too late.

"Bloody hell," I mutter under my breath as I watch the overhead display of the elevator count down to zero. I'm tempted to take the stairs to go after her, when I see the numbers increase again. The lift is coming back up.

I rush to tuck my shirt in and take a deep breath as I wait for it to arrive. I'm going to go downstairs and chase after her. If I have to run down one or two blocks in just my shirt and trousers, so be it.

I'm ready for anything, except for the sight that awaits me as the doors slide open.

There she is. My goddess, my queen.

She isn't looking at where she's going, just rushes out and collides into me.

"Oh, shit," she stammers, while trying to steady herself with both hands on my chest.

I loved when she did that earlier too.

"Emily," I say.

She doesn't respond, so I reach for her chin and guide her head upwards.

Those clear green eyes of hers have changed. She isn't the same anymore.

"You've been crying?" It's not really a question. I can still see the tears clear as day.

She stumbles backwards, but my arms refuse to let her go.

"Emily, I'm sorry," I whisper. "I shouldn't have—"

"Ian, let me go," she mumbles. Her voice is flat like I've never heard it before.

Except maybe when she first told me she was leaving.

"I can't do that," I say in a matter-of-fact tone. I'm neither exaggerating nor trying to be dramatic. "I realised just now when I saw you walking away that I couldn't leave things like this."

She frowns and her eyes glaze over with fresh tears before she breaks eye contact. "I don't understand."

"Emily, I have a confession to make."

She's white as a sheet and her bottom lip is starting to tremble.

I take a deep breath and force myself to carry on talking. Never before have I been as scared as I am now. "I know it isn't rational or even remotely appropriate. And I don't expect you to feel the same way... But I love you, Emily. A part of me always has."

A soft whimper escapes her lips, and she stares up at me again. She looks so small, so vulnerable. To know that she's hurting because of me—because of what we did—is killing me.

"You do?" she asks.

I nod. "I didn't mean to hurt you."

"You didn't." She sniffles and smiles briefly again. It only lasts for a moment, but my heart lights up, anyway.

"Please stop crying," I beg, while trying to dry her face with the back of my hand.

"I didn't know, Ian. I thought—"

"Me too."

Although she hasn't said it aloud, the look in her eyes now tells me all I need to know.

How stupid we both were. Dancing around the real issue all this time.

She smiles again and wraps her arms around my shoulders, hiding her face against my chest. A warmth fills me which I've never known. Earlier in my office it was clear that I could satisfy her physically. Now, I hope to do the same emotionally as well.

"I love you too," Emily says. "Always have."

Now I'm about ready to cry as well. But I don't.

Instead, I clear my throat and tighten my grip on her. "Well, isn't that something?"

She pulls back and looks up at me again. I don't wait to find out what else she'll say, instead I lift her up into my arms and plant my lips against hers. Words don't suffice. This is how I intend to convey the depths of my love for her. Every day, for the rest of our lives.

Now that we know where we stand, her kisses taste all the sweeter.

We forget all about the dinner downstairs, or the party, or the rest of it. I carry her back to my office and continue to kiss her like my life depends on it.

Because it does.

Because during those painful moments before the lift opened, I knew that I didn't want to live without her. Not now, not ever.

And now, I've learnt that she feels the same.

EPILOGUE

*** Emily ***

"Do we have everything?" Ian asks as he walks back into my room.

"I think so." I look around the empty space. Only the shabby furniture provided by the landlord remains.

"End of an era," he remarks and winks at me.

He's right. And I'm not even a little sentimental about it. I'd been living in this downtrodden flat-share near Heathrow Airport for a year and a half now. It's close to the office, and within my price range, but those were the only two things it had going for it. Other than that, it's a shit hole and I can't wait to get out of here once and for all.

Ian asked me to move in with him that same night we first got together. It was too early, and a much too impulsive decision to make, so I told him I had to think about it. Plus, I'd already made other plans.

Lauren had asked me the very same thing, and I'd already accepted months ago. The lease on her new shop includes a little flat on the first floor. We were going to be not just business partners, but roommates as well.

In a few short weeks, I've made a complete U-turn from sad single girl, obsessed with the fantasy of dating my boss, to becoming one half of a power couple others could only dream of.

Funny, looking back now that I never once considered that Ian could be thinking about me at least as much as I had about him. Misunderstandings and misplaced assumptions had kept us apart for a whole year since his split from his ex-wife!

But we're going to have no more of that. From now on we're going to be completely, 100% honest with one another. I trust him, and he trusts me.

It's only been a week, but I'm sure he's right for me. The one.

He tells me I'm his, at least as often.

And that is why I talked things through with Lauren the other night. I explained the situation and declined her invitation. Ian's flat was near enough, so commuting to the boutique every day would not be a problem for me.

And I simply couldn't imagine waking up every morning anywhere else than in Ian's arms.

So, on this icy winter morning, I find myself not moving into Lauren's new flat in Teddington, but into Ian's place instead.

He told me life's too short to wait and see. When you're sure about something, you should just dive in head first. No regrets.

I agree. And that's exactly what I'm doing right now, no matter what Lauren or anyone else tells me.

"Let's go," I say with a smile.

Every time I look at him, I feel those same butterflies in my stomach as always. But unlike at the office it's a good sort of nervousness now, because I know he feels it too.

He puts his arm around me as we leave the house and head to his car. He opens the passenger door for me like the proper gentleman he is, then walks around and gets into the driver's seat. I glance back at the boxes and suitcases that contain my life.

"I'm glad you decided to accept my invitation," he says.

"It was an offer I couldn't refuse," I grin.

"Just don't think you're going to get much sleep."

The hunger in his eyes is evident. It may be awhile before we unpack these boxes, as Ian and I will have more important things to focus on once we get home...

* Ian *

Christmas morning.

We've been an item for almost two weeks now, Emily and I. And I couldn't be happier about how things have turned out.

I watch her across the breakfast table, warming her

fingers on a big steaming mug of tea. She's an angel. Long light brown curls frame her beautiful face. Perfect lips purse to blow at the hot liquid, and I'm enchanted all over again.

All the concerns I'd had about confessing my feelings to her turned out to be unfounded. As much as I'd been obsessing about her this past year, she had done the same.

It was bizarre to hear her reasons for keeping her desires to herself for all this time.

She didn't think she was good enough.

Of all things, she blamed her looks. The idea is laughable to me, so I spend every day trying to convince her otherwise.

At the same time, she assuages my own doubts with every smile, every touch. She just needs to look in my direction with those big, green eyes of hers and I'm done for.

We get along perfectly. Our age gap has never been a problem, even back in the office. It wasn't just politeness that made her laugh at my jokes, or ask about my weekend plans. She's always been interested. I just never knew it.

And since she no longer works for me, that final taboo has also been removed. She's my queen, and I'm going to spend the rest of my life spoiling her rotten.

I'm at a point in my life where I'm financially

stable, and in control of my professional situation as well. Meanwhile she's going to work for a start-up with her best friend. Long hours and stress lie ahead for her with this new venture, so I'm going to make sure I pick up all the slack at home.

She will want for nothing. No matter what happens, I'll be here to catch her in case she falls.

"Thinking about something?" she asks, eyebrows raised.

I shake my head and smile. "Just enjoying the view, sweetheart."

But then, I remember what we'd agreed on. Honesty.

Misunderstood intentions had kept us apart all these months. We'll have no more of that now.

I clear my throat and she looks up from her tea again. "I was thinking about how silly we were, both of us assuming the other didn't feel the same way."

She puts the mug down and leans across the table. Underneath, her foot finds my leg and teases me with a gentle caress.

"Yeah, that was pretty silly."

I lean forward as well, and brush one of her errant curls behind her ear, a gesture I craved to perform so many times before. My heart fills with joy knowing I no longer have to suppress any of these impulses.

"If you're about done with breakfast, perhaps I can demonstrate just how silly it was," I add.

She blushes and her breaths speed up ever so slightly. Whatever the future may bring, I know I'll never get enough of seeing her this way.

She's mine and I am hers. Our relationship is rock solid already. We may have only been an item for a very short time, but we've had the two years at the office to get to know each other already.

"We have to go at eleven," she whispers. "Christmas lunch with my parents."

I don't know if she's reminding me or herself.

"That gives us an hour. We have plenty of time."

She giggles and pushes her chair back. "Come and get it then."

I love how her nighty drapes over her feminine curves. Keeping the mystery alive without obscuring too much of what I already know to be there.

I'm on my feet straight away and close the gap between us. In one effortless swoop, I pick her up into my arms.

"Whoa," she squeals.

All those hours spent at the gym have paid off to make me worthy of her affection. Ever since that first time, I've worked tirelessly to make her feel safe, loved, protected.

Her arms tighten around my neck and she surrenders herself to my kiss.

"I love you, Emily," I tell her. "Always will."

She doesn't reply verbally, instead she tells me with

her kisses.

I love you more, her lips appear to say.

When I lay her down in the bed now, her unruly curls fanned out over the pillow, I pause for a moment to admire her beauty. The winter sun is already streaming in through the bedroom windows, but she doesn't ask for the curtains to be pulled and lights to be dimmed. It took a few tries to get to this point, but she's finally comfortable in her own skin.

The vulnerability in her eyes is gone. I've convinced her. Conquered her doubts. Won her complete trust.

"You're beautiful, Emily," I confess as I position myself on top of her. With one hand I cup her face, while sliding the other up underneath the hem of her dress.

She swiftly pushes my boxers out of the way, allowing my cock to spring free and press up against her entrance.

"*You* are," she breathes.

I enter her, overcome by the moment. She's already wet for me, as I am already hard. Although we've got less than an hour to get ready, I don't rush it. I fuck her slowly and deeply and watch how her body reacts to me with every stroke.

Her breaths quicken through parted lips; her eyelids grow heavy as the pleasure builds. I know how she wants it. How to make her body sing for me.

Seeing her this way gives me more satisfaction than any physical stimulation could.

Then, when she looks up at me, eyebrows pulled together in that cute little frown of hers when she's getting close, I find myself utterly lost in the moment. It's beautiful enough to bring tears to my eyes.

I take a deep breath to ask her a question. I don't even know where it came from. It certainly wasn't planned.

"Marry me, Emily."

Her eyes widen, and her fingers dig deeply into my back. I don't slow, nor do I speed up. My arms keep her firmly in place while I continue thrusting into her with perfect rhythm. My movements send her ever closer towards her inevitable release.

"I can't imagine my life without you. Grant me the honour of becoming your husband."

She cries out. Her legs twitch around my waist and her pussy contracts, milking my cock for all it's worth.

"Yes! Yes!"

As hard as I'd tried to hold back, I can't anymore. My cock squirms and my balls tighten. Before I get the chance to stop myself, I've already cum in her and I'm spent.

She pulls me down into her embrace and I'm helpless to fight it. This is where I belong. This is home.

"Did you really mean that?" she asks.

"Every word," I say. "I should have got you a ring, but—" I don't finish my sentence; instead I nuzzle the soft skin of her neck and plant a few gentle kisses behind her ear.

"I don't need a ring. I just need you," she says.

"So, it's a—"

"Yes, of course." She holds me even tighter. Her gorgeous body shifts slightly underneath me. I'm reminded that I'm still balls deep in her, and I haven't gone fully soft. Although we've both orgasmed once already, that has never stopped us before…

"I'm the luckiest man in the world," I say, as I start to move again. "I'm going to ask your dad for your hand today."

She lets out a sweet little moan, and I'm in heaven once more.

We've still got fifty minutes before we have to leave, and we're going to make the most of every single one of them.

fireworks for the Billionaire

CHAPTER ONE

*** Lauren ***

Four days left until our grand opening.

Although I want nothing more than to check my email, the icy winds force me to keep my hands deeply buried in the pockets of my coat. Until I get to safety, that is.

The coffee shop around the corner, with its quirky interior and extensive menu of piping hot caffeinated treats, is the perfect escape from the ungodly weather outside. I'd first found it a couple of months ago when I came down with Dad to inspect the building housing my new boutique.

At that time, I hadn't even signed the lease yet, and look at me now!

"Hazelnut latte, queen size," I say, while rubbing my frozen hands together.

Alice, who works here, smiles at me as she takes my money. "How's work on the shop coming along?"

"Oh, you know. Every day a new fuck-up."

"Ain't that the truth."

I take a seat near the tiny freestanding fireplace in the corner and peel off my gloves, which so far have done nothing to keep me warm. Maybe I should have a cute little gas fire installed at the shop also… No, don't be silly, I tell myself. I'd have to change the layout and there's simply no time!

As soon as the numbness wears off, I've got my phone in my hand and keep tapping 'refresh' over and over. As if that'll speed things up.

But my much-awaited email doesn't appear. Instead, I open WhatsApp and start typing a message to Emily, my best friend growing up and newly appointed business partner.

'Morning, how are the invitations coming along? How many RSVPs?'

She doesn't respond. She hasn't even read the message yet, it seems. I suppose I shouldn't expect her to. It's only eight-thirty in the morning, and on top of that it's the Saturday after Christmas. I can guess what she's up to, and sleep has very little to do with it.

She's been distracted ever since she got together with Ian, her boss at her old job. They're a couple now and I'm happy for them. I have to be; I feel partially responsible for making it happen. But if we're going to be ready on time for the opening, I need her to focus.

In the background, an email notification gets my nerves surging.

This is it.

My heart is hammering in my throat when I click on the subject line—"Tracking Information"—and follow the link to see my much-awaited shipment's progress. I could use some good news.

"Monday?" I exclaim. "Bloody hell, that's cutting it short."

"Lauren!" Alice calls out from across the shop.

Finally! I rush to the counter and reach for the tall takeaway cup with my left hand, while typing a fresh message to Em with my right.

Delivery's coming in on M-

But I don't get the chance to finish it. The second I grab the cup, I feel a warm, much larger hand close on top of mine.

"Fuck me!" I gasp, almost dropping the phone onto the floor.

"In front of all these people?"

I look up at the man towering over me and am lost in the depths of his warm amber eyes. He's a looker for sure. Tan skin, salt and pepper hair, and broad shoulders that appear strong enough to carry the world.

And if I hadn't been so startled by our sudden contact, I might have handled this encounter with a lot more finesse. After the boys I've tried dating occasionally, it's refreshing to encounter a real man.

"Excuse me?" I ask.

"You're excused. May I have my coffee now?" he asks. The crinkles in the corner of his eyes tell me he's got a few years on me. But like a fine whiskey, the extra maturity has only made him more delicious.

I glance down at our hands, which are still holding on to the same cup, and frown. "That's *my* coffee. Alice called *my* name."

"No, I think you'll find that's actually my coffee. But you're welcome to it, if you give me your number."

I frown and open my mouth to say something, but the words aren't coming.

He's very forward, this guy. Usually I'm the mouthy one wherever I go, but right now I just can't think straight. Where's a clever comeback when you really need one?

So, I'm left shaking my head while I wave Alice over.

"Is this my coffee, or his?" I ask.

She takes one look at my flustered face, then focuses on Mr. Tall, Dark & Handsome beside me and grins. "The slip says Lawrence. Sorry, girl, yours is up next."

"Oh…" I loosen my grip on the cup, only to find that he's still holding on tight. "Lawrence, is it?"

"Nice to meet you." His tone has changed from playful to husky, and the way he's staring at me unleashes a swarm of butterflies in my chest. "And you are?"

"Lauren!" Alice calls out, and slides an identical takeaway cup in my direction.

"Lauren," he says slowly and deliberately.

Instantly I imagine him whispering it to me while we're in bed. *Stop it, woman!*

"Hence my confusion," I mutter.

I hate how nervous he makes me. I fancy myself a capable and independent woman, proprietor of my own business, even. And yet, in front of Lawrence I'm all teeth.

* Lawrence *

What a woman. I'd spotted her the moment I walked in, preoccupied with her phone while warming her other hand in front of the fire. I knew that I couldn't walk out of here without trying to start a conversation.

Her long red hair could light up even the dreariest day, as today had been right up to that point. Life can be funny that way. Just at the moment that your reality starts to resemble a dumpster fire, you end up running into the woman of your dreams.

When she blindly raced towards my cup of coffee, I couldn't let the opportunity pass me by. Although I'd presented it as such, placing my hand on top of hers wasn't a happy accident. It was engineered in that very moment I saw the mix-up unfold.

Lauren is still staring at me. Her expressive blue eyes betray a certain intelligence and assertiveness, even if currently she appears to be speechless. It amuses me to think that perhaps I'm the one having that effect on her.

It's more likely she's still preoccupied by whatever news she'd received on her phone, though. I'm tempted to ask what happened, if I could be of some assistance, perhaps.

Then I remember I have my very own shit storm to deal with already.

"Well, looks like I got my coffee as well. Can I have my hand back now?" She blinks at me and I can only smile.

"That's fair," I say and let go of her.

The girl behind the counter gives me a stern look and clears her throat.

"We're not going to have a problem here, are we?" she asks.

I shake my head and wink at Lauren. "All good, right?"

Lauren straightens her back and frowns again. "Yeah, don't worry, I can take care of this one myself."

I'd like to see her try. Undeterred, I finally pick up my coffee and take a tentative first sip. It's searing hot, just how I like it. Now I'm doubly glad to have wandered into this place; the coffee is as good as the clientele.

Beside me, Lauren does the same, when her phone rings.

"Hello?"

I can't hear what's being said on the other end, just that it's another woman she's talking to.

Good. I can't bear the thought of her answering a call from her boyfriend right in front of me. I must figure out if she's single, first of all.

"Yeah, I'll see you at the shop. Okay, I'll be right there."

Lauren nods at Alice and walks out of the door without so much as acknowledging me. I try not to take it personally.

Wherever she's going, it has to be nearby since she's on foot. I'm considering going after her, when I catch the coffee shop girl looking in my direction with one eyebrow raised up high.

"Look—" I lean over to read her name tag. "Alice. I'm not trying to be a creep, but you seem to know Lauren."

Alice shrugs but doesn't betray any emotion. "She's a regular."

I nod and smile. "That's all I needed to know. Because I intend to ask her out when I see her again."

"Good luck with that," Alice says. I can't tell if she's being sarcastic or not, but I don't really care. One way or another, I'm going to make sure I not only see Lauren again, I'm going to ensure she sees me too.

CHAPTER TWO

*** Lauren ***

I gaze up at the facade and sigh appreciatively when I see the sign. Not-so-Skinny is a dream of mine which has materialised after years of planning. Ever since I completed my design degree, I've been working towards this moment, and it's finally here.

If that god forsaken signature collection arrives on time.

A car pulls up beside me and I hear a familiar voice.

"Lauren. Morning!"

I turn to see Emily in the passenger seat, leaning across and kissing that new man of hers. So, that's Ian.

He's hot, I've got to give her that. After all the stories I'd heard, I wasn't sure if she was exaggerating or what, but she was actually spot on with all her observations. The man is a sight to behold.

Not as hot as Lawrence from the coffee shop, though. I try to shake this particular realisation as quickly as it arises. It's not like I'm going to see him again anytime soon...

"Hi, Ian. Nice to meet you." I wave at him through the open car door. "You should be able to find some parking further down the street. Worst case, there's a lot in a parallel road behind Tesco's."

"Thanks, I'll be right back," Ian says.

The way Emily longingly gazes after his car would have you believe that he's leaving for war or something. They're annoyingly in love, those two. No wonder she impulsively agreed to his proposal already.

"Focus, Em. We've got work to do!" I remind her.

"What do you think, huh?" she asks.

"I think we might have a lot of empty racks during opening night."

"About Ian!" she adds.

I suppress a chuckle. "You know, you never thanked me."

"For?"

"For getting you two together."

She rolls her eyes. "Great! Yeah, thanks, Lauren, for the revolutionary dating advice that brought us together."

"I'm only pointing it out." I lean down and struggle to open the icy cold padlock that's keeping the shop's shutter down.

"But what do you *think*?" she asks again.

I finally manage to open the lock. *Must get some antifreeze spray for the locks,* I remind myself.

Em helps me push the shutter up and we step inside, where I finally turn towards her and give her a pat on the shoulder.

"You were right, he's pretty cute, for a forty-year-old," I tease.

Em lets out an exasperated sigh and shakes her head. "Thanks!"

"You're welcome," I respond in a sugary sweet tone. Our exchange has barely finished when the door opens and Ian walks in, rubbing his hands together and blowing some warmth into them.

As much as I'm teasing Em now, I can somewhat see the charm. And when he puts his arm around her and pulls her against his tall, muscular frame, a pang of jealousy hits me. Not because I'm in any way interested in stealing him away from her, but rather because this kind of intimacy and affection has been lacking in my life lately. As cynical as I can be when it comes to love, I'm also kind of happy for her. Getting engaged this early on is still a mistake as far as I'm concerned, though.

You don't have time to date, especially now, I remind myself. I really don't. The most I've attempted this last year were a couple of short-lived Tinder hook-ups.

Ian lets go of her and approaches me with his hand held out. "Let's do this properly now. I'm Ian, nice to meet you."

I nod and smile. "Lauren. I've heard *so much* about you."

Em rolls her eyes and shakes her head at me.

"Likewise. So, you're the one stealing away my employees right from under my nose."

I grin and nod. "Just the one, so far. But, never say never."

He's alright. She's done okay for herself.

"So, what are we going to do in case the collection doesn't get here on time?" I turn to ask Emily. "Do we risk looking like idiots for our opening, or do we push ahead the schedule now while we still have time?"

"Okay, I think I'd better leave you gals to it," Ian remarks.

"Leaving already?" Em complains.

"I ought to check into the office myself. I'll pick you up in the evening." Ian is out the door as quickly as he arrived.

Just as well. I tap my watch to get Emily to focus again. "Oi! Tracking has the delivery pegged for Monday, but you know how unreliable these courier companies can be over the holidays," I remind her. "What do *you* think we should do?"

She thinks for a moment, picks up her phone, and makes some calls while scribbling on the big legal pad she carries around with her.

Meanwhile, I start arranging the various shelves

and racks around the empty space and figure out the placement of the brand new plus-sized mannequins that arrived a few days ago, before mentally putting their outfits together. It's starting to look like a proper shop already. Even if it doesn't have very many clothes in it yet. The vast majority of our collection is stuck in a container somewhere far, far away.

By late afternoon, we've got a contingency in place just in case the shipment gets delayed. Our opening is going ahead as planned, though we might have to limit our planned fashion show to the one-offs and prototypes from my own wardrobe, plus some off-the-rack items sourced from existing brands.

My body is screaming for some caffeine. Knowing that the coffee shop closes soon, I rush to wrap myself up in my winter coat, ready to once again brave the freezing weather outside.

"I'll get us a couple of cappuccinos. Be right back!" I call out after Emily.

* Lawrence *

For the rest of the day, I'm camped out at the coffee shop. I only leave momentarily to pick up my laptop from the car, so I can at least get my emails done while I wait. If Lauren works nearby, I can only hope she will pop in later for another hot drink. That's when I'll make my move.

And if not, I'm already planning to be right back in

this seat tomorrow at eight sharp to catch her then. Does she work Sundays? Only one way to find out.

Luckily my business is such that I'm not needed at the office all the time. And especially not early in the morning.

Actually, if I wanted to, I could have retired years ago and let my staff handle the day-to-day activities of my property empire. But that's just not my style. I like getting my hands dirty occasionally.

Though right now, what I want to get my hands on the most is Lauren. And she hasn't made another appearance all day.

The girl who works here, Alice, keeps stealing suspicious glances in my direction, but I make sure I keep ordering something or other, so she has no justifiable reason to ask me to leave.

I smile warmly at her as she brings me my fourth cup of herbal tea. It's five-thirty and I've had one of almost every flavour by now.

"We close at six," she remarks. "So, you'll have to find another hideout shortly."

"I know you think you're being protective of her, but I don't mean Lauren any harm," I say.

"Whatever you say."

"We could make things a lot easier if you just told me where she works. Because you know I'll find out eventually."

"And what would be the fun in 'easy'?" Alice

grumbles.

She has a point. Easy is boring. I'll get my way eventually.

We're interrupted by a phone call from the office. Yet another property has been flagged for potential foundation issues and as luck would have it, it's nearby. The shit storm never ends.

I check my watch again. Five-thirty-two. "I'm actually in Teddington right now. I'll see if I can talk to someone there. Whose name is on the lease?"

"Baxter," Debbie says on the other end.

Bloody great. He's going to be a pain to deal with. I'll need to employ a certain finesse to ensure he doesn't get spooked and pull out of the lease for breach of contract. Although we get along okay at the club, he's one guy who knows how to separate business and pleasure.

Let's hope the issue resolves itself.

"I'll check in later. Get the surveyor on call, will you? Offer him double his usual fee if he can come in tomorrow." I hang up the phone and sigh.

"How much do I owe you?" I ask Alice, while gathering up my stuff in a rush.

The building in question has only just been leased out, so it's probably still being renovated. If I hurry up, perhaps I can catch the builders before they leave for the evening. Maybe get the whole mess dealt with without even involving Baxter himself.

Alice is still tallying up my bill, when I decide to just leave her a fifty. "Actually, that should easily cover it, right?"

She looks up from the till, flustered, then nods.

"Keep the change. I'll see you tomorrow." Before she gets the chance to respond, I'm out the door and headed around the corner.

* Lauren *

Jesus, it's cold.

Fireplace or not, the shop was nice and toasty and made me forget just how terrible the conditions outside are. It's dark already; has been for a good forty minutes or so. Not only has the wind picked up sometime during the day, the air is damp and heavy with the promise of sleet.

I wrap my arms protectively around myself and rub my arms, but the freezing air still manages to pierce through my woollen coat. I speed up almost to the point of jogging as I turn the corner, only to collide with a rather solidly built male form. Two strong hands end up on my arms, holding me steady.

"Fuck me, I'm so sorry," I stammer.

"What, again?" a familiar voice quips.

I look up right into those same gorgeous brown eyes that have been in the back of my mind all day. I cannot believe it.

"Lawrence? What the hell?" I say.

"I was hoping to run into you again," he says. "Though, I didn't expect it to be quite so literal."

He's so smug. So annoyingly confident. He makes me weak in the knees just by looking at me and I hate myself for it. When did I become such a coward?

"Have you been following me?" I squint at him suspiciously.

"Funnily, not at the moment. I'm actually on my way to a meeting."

"Oh." I sound a bit more disappointed than I was aiming to.

He grins at me. Damn, he's handsome when he smiles. Otherwise, also. The man is utter perfection, just like I remembered. Just my type, so why does he intimidate me this much?

"Why don't we go for a drink after I'm done. What do you say?" he asks.

I want to say no. No, I want to say yes. I don't know what I want, and can't stop myself from staring up at him while my mind tries to process his question. I could think of much worse ways to spend an evening...

In the end, I only utter a single word: "Where?"

"We'll figure it out. Give me your number, okay? I'll call you in about half an hour to confirm." He whips out his phone and wiggles his eyebrows at me expectantly.

A gust of wind whistles around the corner, making

me shiver uncontrollably. My defences are way down already, and getting a drink with Lawrence is starting to seem like a good idea, so long as the pub is nice and warm. I rattle off my digits, he hits the call button, and my phone starts to buzz in my pocket.

"You'd better go warm up," he observes, while resting his hand protectively on my shoulder.

The gesture makes me even weaker. Is this what it's like to swoon over someone?

"I was going to grab a coffee, actually," I mumble.

My lips are numb in the cold and probably a couple of minutes away from turning blue. His look a healthy and warm shade of pink. I wonder what it would feel like to kiss them...

"Good. I'll try to meet you there if I'm done in time."

I want to protest, say I'm heading right back to the shop after, but he rushes off before I get the chance.

What a man. I can't believe I'm going on a date with him after this. Maybe I should flake out before I make a complete fool of myself?

Remembering my jealousy when Ian turned up this morning, I can't help but wonder if his invitation is actually a good or a bad thing. *It's just going to be a bit of fun,* I insist to myself. *I don't have to marry the guy, do I?*

"Alice, hope I'm not too late," I call out once I enter the coffeeshop for the second time today.

"Not yet, no." She grins.

I breathe a sigh of relief. "Two cappuccinos, please."

"Fancy seeing you here again today. Guess who you just missed?"

"Lawrence. I know."

She cocks her head to the side. "He's been here all day waiting for you to turn up again and said he was coming back in the morning. If you want me to get rid of him, just let me know."

I suppress a smile as my heart jumps a few beats. He has? All day, just for little old me?

"No, that's okay. I think he's starting to grow on me."

CHAPTER THREE

*** Lawrence ***

When I arrive at the premises, Simon Baxter is nowhere to be found; neither is there a building crew present. Instead, I'm greeted by a brightly lit, modern-looking clothing shop front which already looks open for business. *Shit.* Baxter won't be happy if I delay his launch.

The only person inside is a young woman in her mid-twenties, who's working on her laptop.

"Hi, I was hoping to speak to whoever is in charge here," I say.

"That'll be me. I'm Emily, how can I help you?"

"Lawrence Taylor. The landlord of this fine building. I don't think we've met before."

She twists her mouth in a slight frown before getting up to greet me. "Well, I wasn't there for the signing, so…"

I shake her hand. Neither was I, actually. The solicitors handled that on their own.

"So, it's designer fashion, basically?" I ask, scanning the sparsely populated racks.

"That's right, yeah. We're planning to open on

New Year's Day. In fact—"

She leans over and rummages around in a stack of papers on the chair beside her seat. "Why don't you drop in? See the place once it's completely finished?"

I nod briefly and accept the invitation she hands me. "That's very kind. I might just do that." I mindlessly turn the heavy card stock over in my hand. So, Baxter is expanding his retail business by entering the high-end women's fashions market. Interesting.

"The more bodies, the better. It all happened rather last minute, so I'm just trying to ensure we have a full house."

"I understand." What I don't understand is how I will deal if there is indeed a problem with the foundations. It won't be possible to get any remedial work on the quiet, especially not with days to spare.

Emily smiles brightly at me for a moment, then folds her arms. "So, you dropped in to…?"

She seems so excited for opening day; I don't have the heart to lay it all out for her. And in any case, I can't be sure if there really is a problem until I get someone to come in and take a look.

"Just to wish you good luck, actually. I was in the neighbourhood and thought I'll see how things are going here."

"Right… Thanks."

"Everything's working okay? Heating, plumbing, electricals? Downstairs as well as upstairs?"

She shrugs. "I think so, yeah."

"Someone back at the office has gone over the paperwork, and it looks like a fire inspection is due, so I'll send in a guy to do that on Monday, if that's okay with you," I lie.

The inspector isn't due for another few months, but a fire safety check seems like a benign excuse to get the structural surveyor through the door. If he finds any serious issues, I can always come clean then.

Fingers crossed Debbie has managed to get a hold of him.

"That's fine. As long as we're all set by the first," Emily reminds me.

She's young, but her demeanour is professional and confident. I wonder if perhaps she's Baxter's daughter. The age seems about right, from what I've heard.

"Well, I best get out of your hair," I say.

She smiles again. "Thanks for letting me know about the fire inspection."

I nod briefly and try not to feel too guilty for deceiving her. It's how the game is played.

"See you around, at the opening maybe."

My phone rings with perfect timing the moment I step outside into the cold again.

"Yeah, Debbie, please tell me you've got good news?" I ask.

"Roger can make it at eleven, on Monday."

"Perfect. I told the tenant a fire inspector's coming."

"Okay, I'll let him know, so he doesn't give himself away."

I put the phone back into my jacket pocket and exhale deeply. My breath condenses against the icy air, leaving a white cloud. Now that that's done, it's time to focus on the more pleasant part of my evening. I'd promised Lauren a drink, and I'd better make sure the arrangements are top notch.

Rather than head to the coffeeshop prematurely, I take a brisk walk in the opposite direction and find my car. As soon as I take a seat inside, I turn on the ignition and instruct the hands-free to dial yet another number.

"Hey, Carl! What will it take for you to get me a nice set of wheels for the evening?"

I pull out of the lot, rushing to swing by home and change into something a little more appropriate for Lauren.

For her, I'm determined to be at my very best.

* Lauren *

Alice is still making my coffees when about seven girls my age walk into the shop while chattering excitedly. I'm about to comment that they're about to close, when Alice turns and greets them with a loud squeal and excited wave.

"You guys! You're early!" she calls out.

I observe as two of them reach over the counter to give her awkward one-armed hugs.

Alice then turns toward me, takeaway cups in hand.

"Here you go, Lauren. Sorry for the wait."

"No problem," I answer with a smile.

"Your friend is probably waiting for her coffee." Alice nods down at one of the cups. "Otherwise I would have asked you to stick around for this."

I raise an eyebrow and turn to watch the group of girls who've pulled up chairs around the same little fireplace I'd commandeered earlier this morning.

"We've got a regular little get together going. Once a week. In fact—" Alice takes off her apron and walks around the counter and approaches the group, who are just now casting off their mufflers, woollen hats, and gloves.

"Guys! A moment of your attention, please," Alice announces herself.

"What's up, Alice?" one of them, a red-cheeked blonde with long curly hair, asks.

"I want you to meet Lauren," Alice says.

"Hi!" Another one of the group sticks out her hand in my direction. "I'm Amber."

"Lauren," I mumble, still confused about what's going on here.

"She's the one I told you about, ladies."

"Oh, you're opening that shop around the corner. Not-so-Skinny, is it?" the blonde asks. "Kayla."

"That's right," I say.

"We've been dying for something like that to open around here," the one who introduced herself as Amber adds.

"Since you're our new neighbour, I figured I'd ask if you want to join our little club, here," Alice says.

I look around the wind-blown, half-frozen faces. They seem like a friendly bunch. And Alice is right, I *am* their neighbour in more ways than one, now that I've moved into the cosy little flat above the shop.

"How do you all know each other?" I ask.

A handful of them start talking simultaneously. I gather it's a weight loss group, but not really, because weight loss is a load of crap and doesn't work anyway.

"It started off that way, but now we basically come here, bitch about life, and drink coffee once a week," a brunette with a pixie haircut says. "I'm Alexis."

"And finish off leftovers from the display case," yet another adds, while giving me the thumbs up.

Alice grins at me. "What do you say?"

I smile back at her, then at the rest of the group.

"Next week, I'm so there," I say.

"Awesome! Welcome to the dark side," Alexis says.

"I'd better deliver this coffee, before Emily wonders where I've disappeared." I point at the two steaming cups waiting on the counter.

"Actually, why don't you bring Emily along next week?" Alice says.

"I'll ask her, but she's pretty busy with her new boyfriend nowadays." I still can't bring myself to refer to Ian as her fiancé. It's all happened so quickly!

"Boo!" the group complains. "Chicks before dicks!"

I snort.

"Now don't scare her off straightaway, you man hater." Kayla prods Alexis in the ribs with her elbows.

"I'm just sayin'."

"I agree with that, actually," I say, grinning widely. "Bye now!"

"Bye, Lauren," the group calls after me.

I button up my coat all the way and wear my gloves again before picking up the two cups and heading back into midwinter. By the time I'm back at the shop and halfway through my cup of coffee, my phone rings. It's Lawrence.

A sudden wave of excitement and optimism hits me when I hear his voice again. Perhaps it's time to stop being such a spoilsport and just go with the flow already.

"Hi, yeah, I'm still free. Seven is fine by me, but you'd better be taking me someplace warm!" I threaten.

"Don't worry, I won't let you freeze to death on

my watch," Lawrence says.

I suppress a smile. Something tells me that indeed he won't. He's got that playboy confidence in his voice, yet I'm somehow convinced I'll be in good hands with him.

Emily looks up from her cup and gives me a questioning look.

"In that case, it's a date," I say. Remembering that I don't know him well enough to share my home address just yet, I add: "I'll meet you outside the coffee shop at seven."

I hang up the call and sit back with a dumb grin on my face.

"You're going on a date?" Emily asks. "With who?"

"Oh, just some guy I met at the coffee shop this morning." Although I play it cool with Emily, I know Lawrence is far from *some guy*.

"Seriously! That isn't the Lauren I know and love."

I stick my tongue out at her. "You think you're the only one allowed to find herself a man, huh? Give a girl a chance!"

"Fair enough. Just be safe, okay?" she says.

"I'll share my location, just in case."

She nods. "Good."

Looking down at myself, I realise that perhaps I should make an effort to get ready. The boyfriend jeans and oversized loose knit sweater I'm wearing aren't doing my figure any favours.

"Oh, I totally forgot to tell you." Emily stops me. "There was someone here earlier. The landlord, actually—I forgot his name. Taylor, something."

"What did he want?" I ask.

"He's sending someone over tomorrow for the annual fire safety inspection."

I nod, but my mind is a million miles away. "Okay, cool."

"Go ahead upstairs, Lauren. I'll lock up when Ian gets here. You just get ready."

"Thanks." I blow a kiss in her direction and quickly head out and up the steps leading to the flat upstairs.

Excitement about tonight is building fast. Time flies while I take a quick shower, shave my legs, and pick out something nice to wear. Before I know it, seven o'clock is here and it's time to leave.

I take one final look in the mirror on my way out. Pretty decent, even if I say so myself. The figure-flattering fine-knit dress I've chosen for the occasion is part of my own collection. Although I've had it made in a more sedate grey and black combination as well, I've picked the red and maroon variant for myself. Together with the elegant long overcoat and stiletto heeled boots, I almost look like a model from my own catalogue.

This isn't a blind date. Lawrence has seen enough

of me to know what I look like. If he didn't like my curves, he wouldn't have asked me out in the first place, right? So, why hide behind oversized clothes, when I can flaunt it... He can either take it or leave it.

My phone rings as soon as I reach the corner. I assure him I'm on the way.

The icy winds have a way of making me regret my decision of not sharing my address with him both times he called. My knees are frozen by the time I get to our agreed on meeting point.

Although I'm not big into cars, I recognise the waiting vehicle as a Maybach S-Class.

Jesus, who is this guy?

The rear door opens as soon as I approach and Lawrence steps out.

"Lauren. What a sight for sore eyes you are! You look radiant."

I smile, but I'm still speechless, seeing the car. Did he rent it just for this date? This sure is a change from all the losers I've matched with on Tinder lately.

"Get in, it's nice and cosy, as promised," he adds.

I slip onto the soft leather and breathe a sigh of relief when the warmth of the heated seat starts to penetrate my coat.

He gets in from the other side and turns to face me.

"I'm glad you accepted my invitation," he says.

Am I mistaken or does his voice sound even sexier

now that we're alone? He's as handsome as I remember; more so now that he's wearing a form-fitting black suit and crisp white shirt that's unbuttoned at the collar.

"So am I," I whisper, stealing a glance at the little hint of dark brown chest hair peeking up past his shirt. Oh, God, how am I supposed to resist all this?

He smiles widely, revealing a row of perfect white teeth, and all remaining reservations I've had about him seem to melt away. He might be confident to the point of arrogance at times, but why wouldn't he be? He's obviously successful, as well as bloody gorgeous.

And the way he looks at me has my insides all twisted up in knots.

I glance ahead at the uniformed driver, who has kept his eyes fixed on the windscreen throughout.

"We can go now," Lawrence says, raising his voice slightly.

"Yes, boss," the driver answers, and immediately the car starts gliding silently across High Street.

This isn't my first time in a nice car, obviously; Dad has a whole stable of them. Nor is it my first time being chauffeur driven. Lawrence's money shouldn't impress me much, and it honestly doesn't, but it does make me feel strangely at home.

It is however the first time I'm finding myself in close quarters with a man who looks at me like *I'm* the star of the show. Who's pulling out all the stops to make me feel special.

"This is the latest model," I mumble to myself. Dad was planning to order one as well; I remember the brochure on his desk.

"Sorry?" Lawrence asks.

I look up from the soft leather seat and focus on his gorgeous face again. "Nothing. Where are we going?"

"Dinner."

I'd come out tonight expecting a pint at a local pub. Now I'm extra glad I decided to change out of my jeans.

"So, if you don't mind me asking, what do you do, Lawrence?" I ask.

He grins and offers me a glass of champagne. "I own a bit of property around town."

"I see," I remark, while raising my glass in his direction. "I work in a shop. Cheers."

I steal another glance at him before taking the first sip.

It's not technically a lie; it's what I tell everyone on a first date. My family name and implied wealth has perhaps been an even bigger obstacle to my love life than my lack of spare time.

Most guys get intimidated when they find out how loaded my family is. It crushes their ego. That's why my past relationships hardly ever made it past the casual stage.

But Lawrence is unlike anyone I've ever been out with. That can only be a good sign.

CHAPTER FOUR

*** Lawrence ***

So far, so good.

I'd wanted to impress Lauren, and I seem to have succeeded. She keeps shooting glances in my direction while we complete the obligatory small talk and finish our first glass of champagne.

Carl did well to get me this car at such short notice. Her face when she first got in was priceless.

But material things can only get you so far with a woman like Lauren. I'm dialling my charm up to eleven just to make sure she doesn't lose interest. I'm more certain now than ever that I have to win her over. She's turned my world upside-down from the first moment I saw her.

My reaction to her at the coffee shop was primal, like I knew instinctively that she was the only woman for me. When my eyes focused on her, our surroundings seemed to fade. Instinctively I knew that I should make it my mission in life to see her smile.

And how my heart twisted in my chest when I saw her shiver when we bumped into each other outside. I was overcome by a kind of protectiveness I'd never felt for another person. My line of work requires a certain self-assurance, bordering perhaps on selfishness. But our little encounters so far taught me what it feels like to care.

We share a few jokes on our way to dinner; she seems to be in tune with my sense of humour, which can border on crude sometimes. Our earlier interactions had suggested to me already that she doesn't mince her words.

But as hard as I'm falling, the analytical part of my brain is hard at work in the background too.

There's a certain kind of woman who tends to be attracted by all the shiny stuff money brings with it. You can usually tell rather quickly if that's the case, because the conversation will revolve around only one thing after a while.

But Lauren is different. I can tell she appreciates the finer things in life, even if she's subtle about it. Her wardrobe choice for the night is an excellent indicator. There's something about her that doesn't add up. There's no way she simply works in a shop, as she said.

No one who works a minimum wage job can afford the designer boots she's wearing. Or the diamond earrings that sparkle beneath her ginger locks. Either she has money of her own, or she has someone in her life who likes to shower her with expensive presents.

I shift in my seat uncomfortably at the latter possibility.

"Are you seeing anyone?" I ask, as we pull into the underground parking.

She gives me a disapproving look and purses her lips as though she's choosing her words carefully. I like that she doesn't hide her opinions from me.

"That's a very odd question to ask a girl after she's already going on a date with you."

"True, and yet you didn't deny it."

She leans forward slightly, places her hand on my knee, and looks me in the eye. "You tell me if I am."

There's a sparkle in her eye. So, that's where she's going with her answer.

My heart jumps a few beats when I place my hand on top of hers, but I try not to let it show. "You are now."

Does she realise that she's killing me? Her gaze pauses on my hand as I thread my fingers in between hers, then she looks back up at me. I can't read her expression, but I can feel a slight tremble pass through her skin, as though a part of her is trying to pull away again.

I don't let her, instead I scoot a little closer in her direction. How easy it would be to steal a kiss right here. And I know it would feel spectacular if I did.

She seems willing enough, if her flirty answer to

my wildly stupid question just now is anything to go by. Her lips part slightly, tempting me further.

But this isn't how I want to play this. Instead, I hold my breath and lean all the way across her. A whiff of her intoxicating perfume hits my nose despite my best efforts, threatening to break my resolve, but then I close my eyes for a moment to regain focus. I want this woman like I've never wanted anyone before, and yet...

"We're here," I whisper, unlocking the car door at her side.

* Lauren *

He's going to kiss me, right here in the car! Every one of my senses is heightened at the prospect. My skin is buzzing with excitement, and my heart goes into overdrive when he leans toward me. His musky cologne clouds my mind and soothes every last 'what if' that pops into my thoughts.

But the kiss doesn't materialise. When he opens the car door for me and pulls away, I do my best to hide my disappointment. I'm shocked at the ease with which he's playing with my emotions.

I look briefly into his eyes again, but can't maintain it. The intensity in his gaze is startling. His behaviour puzzles me.

"Where's *here*, exactly?" I ask, upon realising that I'd paid absolutely no attention to where we've been going all this time. How could I, when my co-passenger has been so infuriating to be around?

"The Shard," he says, as if it's the most obvious answer in the world. "There's a lovely restaurant upstairs."

I know it. Dad brought me here once or twice. It's not easy getting a booking at such short notice, especially not on a Saturday night.

Lawrence confounds me. If he's trying this hard to impress me, why didn't he kiss me just now? Wasn't it obvious that I wanted it too?

He all but claimed me with his words during our flirty exchange earlier. Remembering his tone when he spoke is still making me weak in the knees.

Am I seeing someone? *You are now,* he said. *Rawr.*

Maybe this whole date is a set-up.

Is Dad going to jump up from behind another one of these parked vehicles and scold me for getting into a car with a complete stranger? Am I being punked?

Lawrence gets out from his side, walks around to mine, and offers me his arm to join him.

No sign of Dad, or anyone else here. I close my eyes for a moment and just breathe.

His fingers gently graze my chin and I find myself staring up at his deep brown eyes again.

"You're a queen," he says. "I hope you know that."

My self-respect goes out the window when a

pathetically soft whimper involuntarily escapes my lips.

I used to think of myself as a bit of a player as well before today, but he's a master at the game. If I'm not careful, I'm going to end up broken in his capable hands.

He places his arm around my shoulder and guides me towards the lift. I inhale deeply, trying to keep my racing heartbeat under control. Despite the mixed signals he's sending, I do feel safe here with him. Maybe he's taking his time with me because he's trying to be respectful? That's the explanation I *want* to believe, anyway.

When we walk into the flashy restaurant near the top floor of the building, all eyes are on us. Again, this isn't my first time here, but this time—with Lawrence by my side—I have to admit I do feel like royalty.

The sting of my earlier disappointment fades when our conversation picks back up. He tells me more about himself, the few passions he makes time for, outside of his otherwise workaholic lifestyle. I can relate, because I'm equally ambitious when it comes to my business, young as it may be.

The tension between us breaks yet again, only to be amped up higher with every hungry look he shoots across the table. It's obvious that I'm having an effect on him too. The way he watches me while I eat, and occasionally runs his index finger past his open collar, as though he's starting to feel the heat of our attraction.

By the time dessert arrives, I start to actually enjoy my role in this dance of seduction.

"The view from up here is truly spectacular," I remark, while savouring the final bite of dark chocolate mousse.

"You're right, spectacular," he says, without ever taking his gaze off my lips.

I suppress a smile and dab the napkin against my mouth. If he's trying to make me blush, he's succeeding.

"If you want, we can get the viewing platform on the top floor all to ourselves," he adds.

I don't have the heart to tell him that I've been there before, so of course I agree. The view of a lit-up London skyline will be the perfect romantic backdrop to get even closer to him.

I'd follow this man to the end of the world and beyond, just to feel as special as I am right now. I'd do anything just to catch another glimpse of adoration in his eyes.

As soon as I put the napkin down and pick up my purse, he's out of his seat, assisting me with my chair. Lawrence has a rough and playful side to him at times, but right now he's assuming the role of Prince Charming perfectly. His hand rests on the small of my back when we start to walk towards the lifts again and butterflies threaten to escape my chest.

If Emily feels only a fraction of all this for Ian, then I completely understand why she accepted his premature proposal already.

Maybe now Lawrence will finally move in for that kiss.

I can't wait.

*** Lawrence ***

The evening is going exactly as planned. I've wined and dined her and we've even exchanged the obligatory details about our families as well as the rest of our lives.

She's an only child to a single father; her mother passed away when she was only a toddler. That's why at twenty-five, she seems wise beyond her years; she's had to grow up at an early age.

I told her things about myself that even Debbie at the office doesn't know. My irrational dream to cycle around the world one day, for example, which seemed to amuse Lauren greatly. I've even told her details about past relationships which were always doomed to fail.

I confessed that these last few years it has always seemed easier to keep potential partners at arm's length. That during those brief moments outside of work when I craved a more human connection, I turned to affairs of a more casual type.

It didn't seem right to lie, and yet she didn't judge me even once. At least not until I dared to disagree with a political opinion of hers.

We're so closely matched in our view of love and relationships, it's almost scary. Slightly cynical, even if our current infatuation appears to suggest the opposite.

But rather than read anything into it like I normally would, I'm taking it all as a sign that we're meant to be. I'm no hopeless romantic; neither is she. But the way she's been looking at me throughout dinner suggests she sees the same thing I do.

I don't have a lot of people in my life who will oppose me, but even now during this very first date, I can tell she hasn't held back even once. If I say something she disagrees with, she'll offer an opposing perspective without hesitation. Yet we're able to follow up every disagreement with a joke and a smile. After being surrounded by yes-men for so long, she's a breath of fresh air and I'm finding myself falling hopelessly for her charms.

She's strong-willed and sharp, but with a soft and gentle side to her that shines through in her blue eyes whenever she really opens up. A formidable woman, who will challenge me and keep me on my toes. I never knew how much I needed that in a partner. No wonder earlier attempts to date led nowhere. I'd always been too quick to act on the physical, before getting to know my date's heart.

Now, I'm glad I didn't kiss her initially in the car.

By the time we finish dinner and head to the viewpoint upstairs, she has me hopelessly wrapped around her finger. I'd wanted to know her inside and out; that's what this date was all about.

And it's not that I didn't *want* to kiss her before. Every fibre in my body was screaming for me to reach out and claim her already. But I made the right choice. Now, nothing stands in our way, and the moment will be all the sweeter for it.

My hand on her lower back is starting to tingle with anticipation. If we don't move out of view quickly, I'll forget myself and steal a taste of those pretty lips of hers right here in full view of the whole restaurant.

Thankfully, the elevator doors slide into place in front of us, shutting us in. And as I turn toward her, I find her eyes already locked onto me.

I guide her chin upwards, and she blinks a few times. Her expression is unreadable to me, yet the rapid change in her breaths tells me she's equally anxious for what is to come.

When my lips touch hers for the very first time, I can hardly suppress a smile. Fireworks erupt, and I know that there is no other woman in the world quite like her.

Lauren is mine. I'll move heaven and earth to prove it to her.

CHAPTER FIVE

*** Lauren ***

When he kisses me for the first time in the elevator, I realise that my earlier doubts were unfounded. This is the single best moment of my life so far. All those mixed signals I'd had trouble interpreting earlier, they snap into place. He hadn't been trying to play me. Fate had played us both.

We barely spend any time upstairs looking at the view; so engrossed are we with the view of each other. Our lips, hands, eyes; we can't keep any of them to ourselves. I'm so wet for him already. I've never experienced anything like it before.

"You're okay with this, right?" he asks me in between feverish kisses.

They're the sort that take your breath away.

Although I'm not entirely certain what he's really asking, I only mouth my answer: a resounding 'yes'. Lawrence immediately leads me back into the elevator for a more extensive make-out session. His strong hands press me up against the smooth metal of the cabin as he devours not just my mouth, but my cheeks, as well as the side of my neck and my cleavage. Never have I been swept up in this much passion.

Nobody has ever made me feel like this. I'm tempted to hit the stop button and rip his clothes off right here.

Sex is easy. With the likes of Tinder, it can be had almost at any time with any number of willing participants. I should know; it's my usual M.O. But this right here is something else.

There's a depth of emotion attached to our encounter that I've never experienced before. He's everything I never even knew I need in my life. Saying yes to this date tonight was the single best decision I've ever made.

My mind fogs over while still in the elevator. I hardly realise what's happening by the time we arrive at a reception desk, where a perfectly dressed man presents us with a key card to a room.

The door closes behind us and I find myself completely alone with Lawrence. The view out the huge window rivals the cityscape we'd just ignored upstairs.

Tonight is going to be a night to remember. A story which—censored for propriety—would be worth telling our children and perhaps even grandchildren one day.

He takes his jacket off and approaches. His attention is on me again.

I'm putty in his hands; helpless against his affections. Everything he does to me, I wish I could tell him how much it means to me. I wish I could make him feel the same. But I can't get even a single word out.

Instead, I show him with my own hands, my lips, my eyes, which keep seeking out his.

He lays me down on the large bed and positions himself beside me.

That won't do; I wrap my arm around his side and guide him on top. It feels so good, having his firm body pressed up against mine like this. My hands explore his back and shoulders through the thin cotton fabric of his shirt. He's all muscle.

He smiles against my lips and returns my kisses with renewed excitement.

"You're amazing, Lauren."

"You are."

I gasp when he runs his hand up my thigh. Everything he does sends me closer to the edge of self-control.

"I want you to know, this isn't a one-time thing for me," he says, while leaning down and grazing his teeth across my collarbone. "This is just the beginning."

My eyes snap shut and I seek him out with my mouth again. I drink in his scent, intoxicating as it is. My fingers have a mind of their own, working away at his formerly crisp white shirt. The lipstick stain on the collar reminds me of everything we've already done so far.

But I know there is so much more yet to be enjoyed.

I'm rushing to get his clothes off, but he's more measured in his approach.

His hands take their time, savouring every part of me he slowly uncovers as he pushes up my dress. I can't resist, and arch up against his hand when it nears my crotch.

He curls his finger against the damp lace and I moan in anticipation.

"This is what you want, huh?" he growls, nibbling the sensitive skin at the side of my neck.

I'm hopelessly lost in the moment. Every move he makes, it seems aimed toward my total loss of control.

"I do." My fingers dig into his shoulder, but he suddenly pulls away again.

"Take it off then," he demands.

I bite my bottom lip, almost drawing blood as I watch him cast off his shirt.

As good as he looked with his clothes on, he's quite a sight naked as well. Sculpted muscles as far as the eye can see. A smattering of dark brown hair adorns the centre of his chest. Breath-taking perfection, all within arm's reach.

His brown eyes look almost black in this light. He's staring me down, waiting for me to reciprocate.

I pull the dress over my hips and sit up to remove it completely. Although I thought I'd learned to love my body some time ago, a pang of uncertainty still hits when I look down at myself. Sure, I've got curves; but quite a few too many of them. My lacy lingerie can't quite contain it all.

How could a man with the physique of a Greek god possibly desire this?

I glance up at him to gauge his reaction and instantly know I shouldn't have worried.

His eyes are wild with lust, but also strangely warm when he meets my gaze. Lawrence casts off his trousers, revealing even more of his flawlessly athletic body, then gets back on top of me and cups my face.

"You're even more exquisite than I dared to dream," he whispers against my lips.

I moan into his mouth, overcome with the sheer beauty of the moment.

He grinds his thigh against my crotch, sending a jolt of electricity through my pussy, which had so far been painfully ignored. That's all I can take before taking matters into my own hands.

Once I slip my hand inside his boxer briefs and grab my first handful of dick, his self-control goes out the window as well. He gets up on his knees and spreads my legs wide.

"Oh, don't make me wait!" I blurt out.

Lawrence pushes my panties out of the way and grazes past my folds with his fingertip. I'm panting already, and we haven't even got to the main course yet. His thick cock presses against my entrance. I raise my hips to meet him.

When he plunges into me for the first time, it takes my breath away completely. My chest feels like it's about to explode, but still, I dare not break eye contact.

His face is tense; numerous lines have appeared across his forehead as he starts to move. Smoothly and swiftly, he thrusts into me. Again, and again.

Each time he does, my moans grow just a little bit louder.

He fills me so completely. His body moves in perfect unison with mine. And the way he's looking at me; I could swear even our hearts are connected. The butterflies in my stomach haven't stilled even once since I got into the car with him tonight.

I feel the pleasure he feels. He knows how I want it without me speaking a word.

I was right earlier. Sex is easy; familiar. But this is something new. What we share in this very moment isn't just a one-night stand. As I tighten my grip on him, I know that I will never want to let him go. Just the possibility that he wants me equally is enough to blow my mind.

My body starts to tighten; I'm getting close. What greater loss could there be than to let the moment fade so quickly?

"Slow down, I don't wanna—" I grit my teeth together, but it's already too late and I cry out his name.

He feels it too; I can tell. His eyes widen as my orgasm washes over me. His movements speed up just enough; everything is just right. Pleasure courses through me; head to toe, from my heart right to the very tips of my fingers.

I don't know whether to laugh, or cry, I feel that wrung out and spent. Then I see Lawrence's face contort just slightly, as he shudders to a halt deep inside of me. His cock squirms and hips buck against my widely-spread thighs. But I don't let him go; I don't let him move even an inch. So desperate am I to receive everything he has to give.

His eyes open and the love in his eyes threatens to break me.

"That was…"

"Perfect." My voice cracks just slightly.

How could it be? Where did all these feelings come from, in such a short time?

Although we've only just met this morning, I look at him now and feel like I'm with a dear old friend. A best friend. A soul mate?

All the stuff he told me over dinner, it's still fresh

in my mind now, while staring into the depths of his brown eyes for minutes on end. I know this was a first for him, as it is for me. He shared himself with me tonight; not just his body but also his soul. We have bonded over tales of old lovers and dates gone disastrously wrong, over childhood anecdotes and idle dreams for the future.

Even when we disagreed about something, it brought us closer together rather than pull us apart. He's one of a kind; the sort of partner I never even hoped to dream about. *Sometimes you just know.* That's what Dad used to tell me when I asked about Mom and him. It's what Emily said when I questioned her about Ian's premature wedding proposal.

And that's what I'm thinking about now, cradled in Lawrence's strong embrace, damp with sweat, yet unwilling to let go.

It turns out this first orgasm isn't the end of our special moment, but a promise of further reward.

For the next hour or so, we take each other in every way imaginable. Me on top, sideways, and finally he even bends me over the edge of the bed. As much as we're lusting for each other, it never feels dirty or out of place. It doesn't feel like *just sex*.

We only stop once I'm sore all over and utterly spent. Too tired to carry on, but unwilling to give up the closeness of his being for the rest of the night.

COFFEE & CURVES 0-2

*** Lawrence ***

Her beauty takes my breath away. So feminine; so soft. She's a goddess among women, every inch of her creamy white skin more perfect than the last.

Lauren turns onto her side and looks at me through her thick black lashes.

It's been a long time since I've seriously gone on a date with a woman; recent attempts always failed at the first hurdle or began and ended with meaningless sex. When you're living and working at the level I'm at, it's rare to find someone you can have a proper conversation with, yet who doesn't seem to just be after your money. And Lauren is one in a billion. A unique specimen. If she allows me to spend the rest of my days worshipping her, I'll be the happiest man alive.

"What are you thinking about?" she asks lazily.

"About how lucky I am to be here with you right now."

She chuckles. "You're such a charmer."

"Only because it's true."

Her hand reaches for me and I catch it mid-air, pulling her tightly into my arms. My fingertips instinctively find comfort in the softness of her hair.

"Tell me," I start.

She tightens her grip on my side and snuggles against my shoulder. "Yeah?"

"What do you do, really? Because you sure as hell

don't just work in a shop."

She laughs. "It's true, I promise! It's right around the corner from the coffee shop."

"Liar."

"I'm not kidding. It's called Not-so-Skinny. Though technically, we don't open until next week."

As soon as she says the name of the shop, my brain starts working overtime again. I recognize the name; I'd only just visited the place a couple of hours ago.

"Not-so-Skinny. Women's fashions," I remark.

"*Plus-sized* women's fashions," she corrects me. "My own designs, actually. I own the shop."

"Small world," I say. "That's where I was headed in the evening for my meeting. I'm—"

Lauren pulls back and leans up on her elbows. "Oh, you're the landlord! Emily mentioned something about you coming over."

I nod.

She chuckles awkwardly. "Wow, talk about coincidences. Things are falling into place now."

"I thought it was Simon Baxter's shop," I mumble.

She nods and her smile fades a little. "Kind of, I mean, I'm his daughter."

Fuck.

I sit up in the bed and try to make sense of what just happened. This beautiful, intelligent and capable woman I've just spent the past hour and half doing naked acrobatics with is Simon-fucking-Baxter's only daughter. Her story about it being just her and her father most of her life makes sense now. Baxter's wife—Lauren's mother—passed away two decades ago. The horror of her revelation must be written on my face, because her next question hits right to the core of the matter.

"Don't tell me you know my dad?" It's not so much a question as a statement; her tone is flat.

I glance over at her, and try to ignore the sharp pain piercing my chest. The shock in her eyes matches my own.

"He rents a few other properties from me," I explain.

Although I try to sound casual, I'm anything but. I don't mention just how many of the same circles we move in. The club memberships, the business lunches, and games of golf. It's a fucking miracle I've never been introduced to her before.

There aren't many rules in dealing with a man like Baxter, but there's one thing you should never do. And that's fuck with his family. Especially, literally.

I'll need to do quite a bit of damage control to ensure he doesn't see our relationship as an insult. My mind is running through a million and one scenarios and ways to spin this, when Lauren breaks the silence.

"I guess this was a bad idea, huh?" she speaks softly as she pulls the Egyptian cotton covers up to her neck and looks away.

The finality in her words cuts me deeply. So, that's it. She doesn't even want to try and make this work.

I'd vowed earlier that I would do everything in my power to make her smile. And instead, she looks like she's about to cry. My own heart aches like it never has before.

Coincidence brought us together so we could share this one beautiful evening. We fit like two sides of the same coin and our parting is equally painful. When she leaves without saying another word, I feel like a part of me has been ripped away which I'll never be able to replace.

I know I'll never find another woman like her. Lauren was the one for me, and now she's gone.

CHAPTER SIX

* Lauren *

The Baxter family curse strikes again.

Lawrence was the perfect guy, or at least he had been right up to the point when he realised who I am. Distraught doesn't quite cover how I feel. I'm devastated.

The look he gave me when he found out who my dad is crushed my heart to a pulp. Just how in the world he managed to worm his way in there in just one evening, I'll never know. He was the first man to ever do so.

It was a cruel twist of fate that made all this happen.

Before we arrived for dinner I'd wondered if I was being played. Turned out I was, but not in the way that I was expecting. Lady luck has really done a number on me.

If there is a lesson in it, I'm not quite sure what it is yet.

There is no hope? You'll never find love? You should change your name and move to another city, and lose the only family you have left, all in a desperate attempt to get a man?

But I don't want or need just *any man*. If this is what I get for daring to hope, then hope is overrated.

Ugh.

Thankfully, I have my work to keep me occupied during the Sunday following our disastrous date. More obsessed than ever, I'm tracking that shipment that will make or break our inauguration event. It's supposed to reach Frankfurt today. If I have to hire a van and pick it up from there myself, I'm ready to do that as well.

Anything to keep me from thinking too much.

My phone rings again. Lawrence. I should block his number, but I don't even want to look at his name long enough to figure out how to do that. Whatever he has to say, I don't want to hear it right now. His reaction last night told me everything I needed to know. It was all too good to be true.

"You okay?" Emily asks, resting her hand on my shoulder.

I shrug. "We've got work to do."

"Yeah… but if you want to take some time for yourself, I can handle it."

That's exactly what I'm trying to do here; this shop is my life. I've lived and breathed this project for years; long before Emily came onboard with me. Before I even found this location with Dad. It has been a dream for as long as I can remember; I can't pull back from it when I'm almost at the finish line.

The fact that Lawrence owns this building has soured things for me but I've always aimed to be a practical, grounded person. It's too late to look for a new place now after all we've put into it. Emily can deal with him going forward, so I don't have to.

I shake my head. "How many people have responded to the invitation?" I ask.

"It's eleven in the morning on a Sunday. Nothing has changed since the last time you asked me that," Emily responds.

Right.

"Let's go over the food, then. And show me the pictures you like for the projector slideshow."

Emily sits down next to me and takes my hand. "How about a nice, hot cup of coffee, huh? And then, why don't you tell me exactly what happened last night?"

I want to protest, and get her to just answer my questions, but actually she's right. I'd love a coffee.

"I'm not going to the coffee shop," I mumble.

What if Lawrence is hanging around, waiting to talk to me? Sure, he could just turn up on my doorstep if he wanted to, but something tells me he wouldn't disrespect my privacy like that. Not after I've been ignoring his calls all night. The coffee shop is a neutral ground, though.

"No, silly! I'll get us the coffee. You just wait here,

okay?" Emily says. "We'll talk when I get back."

I merely sit there and watch as she heads for the door. The last thing I want to do is *talk* about it. Especially with Em, who firmly has her rose-tinted glasses on ever since getting together with Ian.

"Oh, Em!" I call after her.

"Yes?"

"If you think we could use the extra people, why don't you give some invitations to Alice. In case her friends are interested. Tell her I said *the more the merrier.*"

"Sure thing."

I sigh and lean back in my chair. When I remember Alexis' *chicks before dicks* comment, a brief smile breaks through my otherwise cold facade. They seemed like a nice bunch, and exactly the kind of energy I need in my life right now. It would be good if at least some of them can make it.

* Lawrence *

It's been days since I've been to the office. Debbie is under strict instructions to hold my calls, and as a result my phone has been eerily silent throughout. She knows better than to go against my wishes, especially when I'm in a mood.

And 'a mood' doesn't quite describe the pit of despair I've found myself in. I haven't eaten; I haven't slept. All I've done is relive Saturday night and tried to reach out to Lauren.

The only interruption to my endless brooding has been a call at eleven-thirty on Monday. Roger, the surveyor, called with the results of his inspection.

Lauren's building is safe. It was all a false alarm. Her shop opening can go ahead as planned, and I can't even tell her, because she never knew about this potential disaster. Not that she's accepting or returning any of my calls, no matter how many voicemails I leave her...

For the rest of this day as well as the next, I keep going over the events of Saturday night, to figure out what I should have done differently.

Lauren is Simon Baxter's daughter. That, I cannot change. But my reaction to that revelation could have been much, much better. If only I'd offered some words of encouragement or some willingness to move past it together. I could have suggested that Baxter wouldn't disapprove if we presented our relationship to him in the right way. I did none of that.

Despite appearances, I am serious about Lauren. She made me feel like no other woman ever has. I'm not sure what love feels like, but perhaps this is it? Right up to the moment she turned her back and walked away. It crushed me to watch her leave in silence.

I should have stopped her, should have insisted that she talk things through with me.

Oh, who am I kidding? She knows her father better than anyone. She left because she didn't want to date one of her dad's friends or associates. There's no chance in hell for the two of us.

Baxter would rip me a new one if he found out as well. He's not just shrewd in business; he's relentless. Good qualities for an ally, but as an enemy? Deadly.

Are my feelings for Lauren worth ruining my business over? The one I'd spent the best part of my life to build from the ground up? Could I give up everything for her? Because that's what might it come down to in the end...

When my phone rings again on Tuesday—a mystery number—I don't have the mental energy left in me to answer. It's probably a last-minute New Year's Eve invitation I have no intention of accepting.

I let it ring and ring, but then curiosity wins out just before it switches to voicemail.

"Hello?"

"Hi, it's Emily, from Not-so-Skinny in Teddington. We met on Saturday? Hope I'm not disturbing..."

What the actual fuck? My grip on the phone tightens until it makes an ominous crunching sound.

"Are you still there?" she asks.

Part of me feels like hanging up and smashing the phone against the wall. Of all the people in the world, why on earth is Lauren's business partner calling me?

And on New Year's Eve, of all days?

I grit my teeth and force myself to take a few deep breaths. My heart races so fast, I could swear she'd be able to hear it over the phone.

There has to be a perfectly reasonable explanation. She probably just wants to discuss Roger's visit.

Focus!

"Hello?"

"Yes. I'm here," I say.

Nothing could prepare me for the conversation that follows.

CHAPTER SEVEN

* Lauren *

This should be the happiest day of my life.

I look around the tastefully decorated boutique, but I can't muster even an ounce of excitement. Emily picked up the slack these past couple of days. Although I spent every waking moment in here, trying to focus on work, my attention has been all over the place. Something which she had to gently remind me of regularly.

Now it's all ready. The collection arrived only slightly late, so we managed to fill the racks with minutes to spare.

The caterers are setting up already, and the few models we managed to book at such short notice are getting changed in the store room. Everything has come together, but I'm in no mood to celebrate.

"Lauren!" Dad walks in with his arms wide.

I close my eyes and sigh deeply when he hugs me. It's been him and me against the world for most of my life. Looks like that's the way things are meant to stay.

"What's wrong, darling? Nervous?" he smiles.

"Oh, hi, Emily. Have you been working my little girl too hard?"

"Hello, Mr. Baxter," Emily responds. "You know as well as I do that no one can make Lauren do anything she hasn't already set her mind to herself."

She shoots an encouraging smile my way.

He lets out a hearty laugh. "True enough."

I mouth a 'thank you' at Emily for not sharing the true reason behind my fragile mood. Of course, I'd tried my best not to tell her either, but she managed to pry it out of me anyway. Enhanced interrogation is one of Em's specialities.

Dad pats me on the shoulder to get my attention again. "Well, sweetheart, why don't you show me around? Once the rest of the guests turn up, you'll be too busy to entertain your old man."

I swallow the lump in my throat and guide him past the various displays, pointing out the highlights of my very first winter collection. A glimmer of pride starts to build while I show him everything, but I can't hang onto it long enough to shake my melancholy.

"Good job, Lauren. A chip off the old block."

"Thanks, Dad." I smile up at him, but my heart isn't in it.

From the concerned look he's giving me, it's obvious that he can tell.

"Break a leg." Dad squeezes my shoulder. "I'll be

around if you need any help."

I turn to face the door and blink away the onset of tears. This isn't how I'd imagined my opening would go.

But within minutes, I'm too busy to dwell on my feelings anymore. People are starting to pour in. Looks like Emily's hard work has paid off; the guest count is growing steadily and I'm seeing plenty of familiar faces.

"Hi, Lauren!" Alice waves at me as she enters along with a handful of her friends. "Alexis is sorry about not making it, she has to work tonight."

I'm immediately surrounded by Amber, Kayla, and another girl I recognise from the coffee shop, Megan.

"Welcome! Thanks so much for dropping by. Why don't you help yourselves to some bubbly," I say with a fake smile plastered on my face.

They take turns hugging me, then attack the finger food. Tasteful music starts to play, and I breathe a sigh of relief. If I can get through the rest of the evening without falling to pieces, perhaps there's hope for me yet.

I sneak a sip of champagne myself, and almost choke on it when I see the one person I never expected to lay eyes on today. The shop is so crowded I only catch a glimpse of him through the glass frontage. As soon as I do, everything else fades into the background.

I wish the ground would swallow me up so I wouldn't have to face him. Not tonight. Not in front of Dad and everyone.

But rather than walk away like he should, he steps up to the door and enters. My eyes start to sting again. I hold my breath just to stop myself from screaming and making a scene.

God, he's handsome. Why does he have to be so bloody handsome?

Even more than that, the look in his eyes shakes me to my core. There's that same hunger I saw on Saturday, of course. But also something else. A vulnerability, perhaps even a weakness I didn't know he possessed.

A warm hand rests on my shoulder and I wince internally.

"Surprise inspection, Lawrence?" Dad's attempt at a joke.

But neither of us can muster a smile.

"Not quite. Good to see you, Simon," Lawrence says.

My knees threaten to buckle underneath me at the sound of his voice. Memories of Saturday night flood my mind. Everything—every part of ourselves that we shared, until it all came to an end.

"What are you doing here?" I ask. It comes out a lot harsher than I had planned for.

"You two know each other?" Dad asks.

I blink a few times and take a deep breath while ignoring the question. *Oh, Dad, you have no idea.*

"If you're insisting on staying, let's at least talk somewhere more private?" I snap.

Lawrence shakes his head and only now do I see that his eyes are glazed over as well. I'd taken him for a man who never shows weakness, but this is his low point as well as mine.

"No." He turns towards Dad. "Actually, Simon, it's a good thing you're here for this."

Lawrence reaches for my hand. I'm in complete shock and helpless to stop it.

My eyes snap shut involuntarily when I feel the warmth of his fingers against mine. I have no self-control when it comes to this man. No self-respect left.

"Lauren. From the moment we first met I knew you were different."

"The fuck's going on here?" Dad grumbles while tightening his grip on my shoulder.

I let out a pathetic sob.

"You're one among billions. Every time I see you, you brighten my world. I know that I've hurt you and that's unforgivable, but I hope you'll give me a second chance. I'll spend every day of my life making it up to you. Trying to convince you that you're the best thing that's ever happened to me. That nothing else matters to me, except seeing your next smile."

Dad takes a step forward, his fist tightened into a ball. "What's going on between you and my daughter?"

Silent tears stream down my face.

"If you come after my family, it means you come after me. She's all I have in this world. I'll go to any lengths to protect her from the likes of you!" Dad continues.

"Dad…" I whisper. "Dad!"

His head snaps in my direction.

"Let's take this outside, okay? Let's not do this here in front of everyone," I beg.

Dad's face is turning red and that one vein in the side of his head is starting to throb like it does when he's really enraged. He's always been short-tempered. *Fuck,* I hope this isn't going to turn physical.

The three of us silently walk out onto the street. As soon as the doors shut behind us, Lawrence starts to talk again.

"Simon, I know this isn't what you want to hear, but I love her. I've never been as certain about anything in my life."

I choke back further tears and wrap my arms tightly around myself.

"I'll destroy you. I'll destroy your business. Everything you've worked for, kiss it goodbye right now," Dad threatens.

Lawrence's eyes are on me. He tilts his head to the

side and forces a sad smile.

"Lauren." His voice cracks slightly as he says my name. It gives me shivers all the way down my spine.

"Yes?" I say, but no sound comes out.

He gets down on one knee and holds a small jewellery box in my direction.

"Please accept my apology. I'll always love you, Lauren. I'll take care of you; will work tirelessly to give you everything—"

Dad takes a step forward and grabs Lawrence by his collar. "Get the fuck away from her! She obviously isn't interested!"

"Stop! Jesus, will you both just stop for one fucking second!" I scream.

Both of them pause, their eyes fixated on me. Meanwhile, I'm shaking uncontrollably. What the hell just happened? Has Lawrence seriously decided to commit career suicide tonight? For me? The gravity of the situation is starting to sink in, and it's turning my knees to jelly.

Dad, of course is just being Dad. He's trying to look out for me, but in this instance, he's not helping.

"Dad." I sniffle. "Dad, please let Lawrence go."

He does, and his eyes soften when they train on me. "Lauren, you can't seriously expect me to stand by and watch while this—this motherfucker—" He takes a few deep breaths in an attempt to calm himself.

It's not working. The vein on his temple is still throbbing furiously.

"I love him too, Dad."

Lawrence's shoulder slump forward in relief and a more genuine smile breaks through his previously bleak expression. My heart skips a couple of beats at once.

"You're not serious!" Dad demands.

"I am."

"This fucker's the reason you were so upset these last few days! You didn't even come over to see the fireworks at New Year's Eve like you normally do," Dad continues. "I thought you were busy preparing, but you weren't, were you? You were upset because *he* hurt you!"

"It was a misunderstanding. Please just let it go. Let us figure this out together, okay, Dad?" I plead.

I glance down at Lawrence, who thankfully has decided to keep quiet for the moment. Nothing he could say right now would help, anyway. He strikes a miserable figure, out here in the cold. This grand display wouldn't have been easy for a proud man like him.

I look up at Dad again, whose expression calms further when he meets my gaze. Puppy eyes have always worked a little too well on him.

"Of all the men in the world, *this* is the one you want?" he asks at last.

I try to ignore the judgement in his tone.

"Yes, he is. It's like what you used to tell me about Mom and you. When you know, you just know, right?"

He sighs and shakes his head.

"Please get up," I tell Lawrence. "You're kneeling in a puddle."

"At least accept the ring," Lawrence says. "Who knows, it might be all the wealth I'll have left after your father gets done with me."

I chuckle through my tears as he takes it out of the box and puts it on my finger. A blue sapphire; princess cut. When he gets back up, I wrap my arms tightly around his neck. The warmth of his body against mine makes me realise just how cold I'd been up to this point. The freezing air stings against my cheeks, but I can't stop smiling.

"Thank you for not giving up on us," I whisper.

Dad's reputation had scared off numerous potential boyfriends in the past. Every time I'd come home heartbroken, he'd reassure me that they just weren't worth it. That I was better off without any of them.

But Lawrence didn't back down like all the others. He came here and faced Dad head on, no matter the consequences. It was the most romantic thing anyone has ever done for me. The beautiful ring is just the cherry on top.

"Let's go back inside. Your guests will be wondering what's going on," Dad grumbles, as he backs away from the two of us.

"You go ahead, Dad. I'm going to need a moment," I respond.

Lawrence pulls back from our embrace and dries my tears with his sleeve. The way he's looking at me now is enough to almost make me cry again. But this time, they're happy tears.

"My makeup must be a complete nightmare," I mumble, while trying to dab at my lower eyelid.

"You're still the most beautiful woman I've ever seen," Lawrence says.

"Such a charmer," I tease.

"Do you think he'll ever accept me as your partner?" he asks, his expression turning thoughtful as he watches Dad return to the party inside.

I grin up at him, cup his face and guide it down towards me. "There's a secret about Dad that most people don't know about."

"Oh yeah?" Lawrence's hot breath tickles my lips.

"He can't say no me. He might try, but in the end, I always get what I want."

When our lips fuse, my heart rejoices. This is what I've wanted, what I've *needed* all this time. So many things remain unspoken between us, but it doesn't seem to matter much anymore. He's proven beyond any shadow of a doubt that he's as hopelessly lost in our affair as I am.

We might have only gone on one date so far, but with nothing standing between us anymore, I know this is only the start of something much bigger. The future is ours.

"I love you," I whisper. "I don't know how or why, since it all happened so fast. But I do."

"I love you too."

EPILOGUE

* Lawrence *

Five years later.

As I watch Lauren with our three-year-old, Spencer, a familiar warmth fills my chest. I'd never considered myself to be capable of becoming a family man in my younger years. My sole focus had always been on work; relationships seemed like an unwelcome distraction.

But that was before I met her.

The moment I laid eyes on Lauren in that quirky little coffee shop in Teddington, my entire perspective started to change. She taught me things I didn't know I needed to learn.

She showed me how beautiful and fulfilling life could be when you have someone by your side to share it with.

I thought that was it, the pinnacle of happiness. Little did I realise there was another, equally intense kind of love reserved for this next generation. The joy you feel when your child smiles at you is unmatched by any other feeling I know. I now live not just for Lauren, but for Spencer as well. Two people in this world to keep me grounded and remind me daily that there is something larger than just myself out there. Something worth protecting and fighting for.

Thankfully little Spencer takes after Lauren. I can't suppress a grin when I see some of Lauren's features reflected back in his little face.

He's been the Christmas miracle to finally get Simon back on good terms with me.

Although Lauren was right that night when I confronted them both—about Simon not being able to say 'no' to her—he wasn't happy about our relationship at first. He kept me at arm's length for the better part of a year.

I can't blame him. Looking at Spencer now, I can understand how protective he must have felt of Lauren when we first got together. I would give my life to keep him safe and happy.

But little Spencer's arrival changed everything yet again; I suppose Simon finally accepted the fact that I was serious about his daughter. That I had truly committed myself to Lauren's happiness.

My moment of reflection is broken when the elevator doors open, revealing a few more familiar faces.

"Em, you made it!" Lauren calls out from the open plan kitchen. "Look, Spence, It's Em and Deedee!"

Spencer squeals at the sight of Emily's little

daughter, Deidre. The exhilaration in his voice is infectious.

"Hi, Emily." I greet her with a hug.

"Ian." I turn towards Emily's husband, who steps out of the elevator behind her. "Good to see you both."

"Likewise. Beautiful clear night tonight," Ian says, while pausing to admire the view from the large windows. Living high up above the Thames does have its perks.

"We should see a good display when the time comes. Drink?" I ask.

He nods, and I pour him a scotch, before refilling my own glass.

It's so cute how these two are with each other, isn't it?" he says. "Cheers."

I follow his gaze towards the two kids, who are holding hands and bouncing up and down in excitement. It makes me smile as well.

"Cheers."

"Lauren's dad didn't make it?" Ian asks after taking his first sip.

I shake my head. "He's taking Kayla to Paris for the holidays. So, it's just us and the kids."

"Nice."

I turn to see what Lauren is up to. She's still in the kitchen, arranging the champagne glasses for later. Now Emily has joined her and they're having an animated discussion about something. Always talking shop, those two.

"Work on the new location is coming along nicely," Ian remarks. "Emily showed me around this morning. Very impressive; only a stone's throw away from Harrods."

I nod and smile. "That, it is. They've done pretty well for themselves, our girls."

Lauren and Emily's business has taken off these last couple of years. My contacts in the property market have helped secure a coveted spot on Brompton Road in Knightsbridge for them. But growing their brand into what it has become—that is all on them.

Ian raises his glass in my direction and grins. "Indeed. I sometimes wonder what use they have for us anymore."

He takes a sip and joins Spence and Deidre, who have settled down on the large shag pile rug by the fireplace. Ian asks Deidre to show him all the toys they're playing with and I watch for a moment. Five years ago, I couldn't have imagined where I'd be right now. New Year's Eve used to look very differently for me back then.

Flash parties, plenty of women, and free flowing alcohol. That was it in a nutshell.

I don't even miss it a little.

"What are you thinking about?" Lauren's voice

brings me back to reality.

Her hand on my shoulder gives me goose bumps.

"I was just thinking about how this new year is going to be the best one yet," I respond, while wrapping one arm around her waist and pulling her closer.

"I agree," she whispers.

I lean down, kiss her sweet lips, and marvel at how she manages to take my breath away even now. Fireworks, just like that very first time.

We can't know what the new year will bring, but I know that I have everything I need right here. She looks up at me, warmth filling those big blue eyes of hers, and I know she feels the same. As wonderful as the past five years have been, the next will be even better.

falling for my friend's Dad

CHAPTER ONE

*** Simon ***

New Year's Day.

"Of all the men in the world, *this* is the one you want?" I ask, glaring down at Lawrence, who continues to kneel in front of my daughter. The whole situation would be hilarious, but this is Lauren we're talking about. I'd lost my sense of humour the moment he stormed into her shop inauguration and made a scene in front of everyone.

Adrenaline is rushing through me. If he gives me even half an excuse, I'll plant one right in his arrogant face. What the fuck was he thinking? He's *my* age almost, and a dog at that. And he's trying to get with *my* daughter. I could kill him right here and feel no remorse whatsoever.

Except…

"Yes, he is. It's like what you used to tell me about Mom and you. When you know, you just know, right?" Lauren says.

When she looks at me like this, with those big blue eyes that remind me so much of Emma, I know I can't refuse her. Emma was the tough one; the one to maintain discipline. I could never follow through once Lauren dialled up the charm.

Some might say I've spoiled my daughter, but I did the best I could. It's hard to accept how much she's grown. To me she's still that same little girl with the ginger pigtails who couldn't understand where her mother had gone when she didn't make it home from the hospital.

I try to get a grip on myself, but the anger is just too overwhelming right now. For all of her life, I've tried to shield her from the ugliness of the world. I never involved her too much in the business either so that she would go out and make her own way in life.

And now, our worlds have come full circle with Lawrence, of all people. Jesus Christ, what are these two thinking?

I glance down at the unfortunate couple again, but their tearful reconciliation is making my stomach turn. The sooner this spectacle ends, the better.

"Let's go back inside. Your guests will be wondering what's going on," I say, in the calmest tone possible under these circumstances.

"You go ahead, Dad. I'm going to need a moment," Lauren replies.

Lawrence gets up, puts his arms around my little girl, and I see red. Best to get away before things escalate. I have Lauren's best interests at heart, obviously, even if she won't see it that way. If I intervene now, she might never forgive me.

This is a mistake she's going to have to make all for herself. I can't live her life for her.

Once inside and among the crowd, I try to focus my attention elsewhere, so I analyse the event at hand.

Lauren and Emily have done an amazing job on this place in such a short time. The shop looks slick; high end, just as Lauren had envisioned. Some of the designs adorning the tastefully laid out racks and shelves remind me of various sketches and drawings Lauren had shown me previously.

Although my connections—namely Lawrence, whom I still want to murder—helped secure this rather reasonable lease, this business is all them. Their planning, their execution. My role was advisory at best.

And this inaugural party—despite its inconvenient timing—looks to be a success. There's a good mix of people in attendance: industry contacts, models, and even some press are represented here today.

"Mr. Baxter." Emily approaches and points at one of the trays of champagne. "Please help yourself."

I force a smile, though I can still feel the adrenaline coursing through my veins. The poor girl has no idea how close I am to throwing the entire tray across the room. But of course, I do nothing of the sort. Lawrence is the one I'm angry with, not Lauren or Emily, and this is supposed to be their night.

"Don't they have anything stronger?" I mutter to myself while taking a first, generous sip.

The quality is appropriate for the occasion as well as Lauren's budget, but it's definitely not high class. I wish I had better options to hand.

The glass empties much too soon, and I'm back to wondering what to do with my hands, just to fight the urge to strangle someone.

Distract and deflect.

I scan the crowd and try to guess at everyone's back story. Some people are very easy to place. The social media influencers who are trying to take the perfect picture to please their followers. The locals who dropped in out of sheer curiosity. A couple of people appear to have attended simply to drink champagne and eat the snacks.

Then, there are the models. I'd spotted a couple of them emerging from the back room earlier wearing some of Lauren's more recognisable outfits.

And finally, I see *her*. She's posing for a selfie with Emily and some other girls I don't recognise; potential customers, maybe? I'm good at faces, and I'm sure I've never seen any of them.

Long blonde hair, tastefully applied makeup and a figure with curves in all the right places. I don't recognise the dress she's wearing, but her look is perfectly put together. Must be one of Lauren's newer designs which I haven't seen before.

My eyes pause on her just a bit too long for comfort. She notices me too, because as soon as she meets my gaze, she smiles and looks away again.

She's yours if you want her. Just why and how that inappropriate thought pops into my head, I cannot be sure.

I like my instincts usually; I rely on them every single day in business. And right now, every fibre in my body is screaming at me to go over there and talk with *her.*

Instead, I turn around and grab a refill of cheap champagne. Again, I wish they had something stronger to kill the anger that still remains.

* Kayla *

When I arrive at Lauren's shop, he's already there, browsing the displays. I'd spotted him the very second I walked in, of course. Closely cropped strawberry blonde hair, broad shoulders, and a broody sort of gaze, as though he has some depth to his character. A darkness, as yet to be uncovered.

I've always had a thing for bad boys—much to my own detriment—but at least this one doesn't look rough, but classy. In any case, there's definitely a lot going on in that head of his, and my curiosity is piqued.

His dress sense is smart. Expensive. He looks

financially secure, one might say, as expected from a man who looks to be in his late thirties, or so. But I can't shake the thought that he might be keeping a dangerous secret. I want nothing more than to find out what it is. And what he hides under that well-tailored suit of his.

"Hey." I prod Alice in the ribs with my elbow. "Check it out."

"Hm?" She turns to see what I'm looking at. "Oh, I see!"

Amber and Megan lean in to join our little exchange.

"I'm calling him, before anyone else does," I say.

"Don't be such a slag. At least check if he's wearing a ring first!" Alice complains.

"That's not fair, I was behind you guys," Amber butts in. "Who are we talking about?"

I grin. "So what if he is? That's his problem, not mine."

Alice rolls her eyes and takes a couple of steps forward to meet our host. "Hi, Lauren!"

I have no intention of going after a married man, if that's what he is. That's more Amber's cup of tea than my own. I'm just teasing Alice, and she knows it. Probably.

I pause for another moment and enjoy the view of Mr. White Collar Crime in the corner, then quickly catch up to the rest of the group, who are chatting to

Lauren already.

The shop looks amazing, admittedly. I tell her so while giving her a little hug. It's only the second time we've met, but Alice says she's cool, so I'm hoping we'll hit it off as well once she starts coming to our weekly get-togethers.

Lauren points to the tray of champagne on the counter, and we waste no time at all before helping ourselves.

"Nice stuff, huh?" Amber remarks, while running her fingers past some of the dresses on the nearest rack.

"Prices are pretty steep," Alice says.

"You want cheap clothes, go to Primark," I say. Maybe once my first month's salary comes in, I'll treat myself with one of these outfits.

She makes a face at me. "I'm only making an observation."

"Maybe if you wear one of these, you'll get better tips at the coffee shop," Megan teases, pointing out a sexy little black number.

We share a giggle and I casually turn around to see what *the guy* is up to. He's nowhere to be seen.

"Well, that sucks," I mumble.

"Hm?" Alice asks.

"Oh, that guy I pointed out. He's vanished into thin air," I say.

"Maybe he noticed your thirsty looks and ran,"

Alice counters.

I stick my tongue out at her. Alice shrugs and walks over to another display. "I like these loose knit sweater thingies," she says, picking one up off the shelf. "Very flattering."

Megan joins her and I'm left behind, wondering if I imagined him. My disappointment fades into the background when Alice introduces Megan, Amber, and me to Lauren's friend and business partner, Emily. We have a few laughs, take a couple of pictures together, and then, much to my excitement, my mystery man reappears next to the finger food display. I can't help but smile when he glances in my direction.

Did he notice me as well? Could I be so lucky?

"He's back," I whisper at Alice. "Don't look!"

Of course, she does look. "Go on then! Talk to him before he *really* disappears."

"You think?"

She gives me a stern look. "You're the one who called him, but now you're having second thoughts? If you don't, then I'm sure Amber will have a go."

I take a deep breath and check myself out in one of the full-length mirrors beside me. Not too bad, if I suck in my stomach a bit. The heels certainly help.

Alice prods me in the back, forcing me to take a step forward.

"Alright, alright! I'm going," I hiss.

Nerves flutter in my chest, making me feel lightheaded. Or is that the champagne? Funny, I'm not usually this much of a chicken shit.

Now or never!

Nobody seems to be paying me any attention as I cross the shop floor and position myself behind my intended target. His cologne knocks the wind out of me. Jesus, he's even sexier up close. And tall, too.

"Hi," I say.

He turns around and meets my gaze. His light grey eyes mesmerise me.

"Hi." He sticks out his hand.

"I'm Kayla."

"Simon."

The feeling of his warm fingers surrounding mine takes my breath away. Approaching this man was either a stroke of genius or the worst idea I've ever had. All I know is, I'm in trouble. The look in his eyes suggests that he can tell.

"I was wondering who would make the first move," he says.

Yup, big trouble.

"So, you did notice me as well," I counter.

We share a smile, but his eyes hide some deeper emotion I can't pinpoint.

"Champagne?" He holds a filled glass in my direction. "I would ask what else you'd like to drink, but, well… Let's make the best of what we have."

I accept it with a nod and a coy smile. "A smarter person would quit before things got out of hand. But, I won't."

His stare intensifies and those butterflies in my stomach are making a comeback.

"I'm sure the proprietors of this fine establishment won't mind you enjoying yourself a little," he says.

"I was told to make myself comfortable, so…"

He nods and raises his glass in my direction.

The champagne cools my suddenly parched throat. There is so much going on in my imagination. So many dirty deeds to fantasise about. And none of it translates into something sensible I could say to him.

CHAPTER TWO

*** Simon ***

As soon as she strikes up a conversation, I'm hopelessly lost in the light-brown depths of her eyes. Kayla is obviously younger than me; perhaps in her thirties? The difference between us doesn't feel insurmountable, though. There's something in the way she carries herself that suggests she's worldly and mature for her years. No wonder, considering the circles she must move in.

She looks upon me like an equal, rather than an authority figure, which is a nice change of pace for me. It's hard to feel a kinship or connection with someone when they keep calling you 'Mr. Baxter' or 'Sir' all day.

I'm sure I'm not the first man to flirt with her at an event like this. Such a cliché; I'm the older rich guy and she's technically the hired help, and yet… I can't help myself. From the moment I saw her, a part of me rose to the challenge.

Throughout our innuendo-filled small talk, she's kind enough to humour me. The way she looks up at me in between sips from her glass suggest she's enjoying the attention.

I'd like to think I notice when people are lying. Those little tells everyone seems to have, spotting them is like second nature to me. She has none. Every little smile she shoots in my direction looks genuine to me.

Normally, I wouldn't do this. I *never* have before. On any other day, with any other person, I wouldn't have had this conversation.

Perhaps it's the mood Lawrence's bullshit put me in that did it. The sudden realisation that I've put my love life on hold for so long, when the entire world—including Lauren—has moved on and rightly so.

Don't I deserve a little something for myself? Kayla's appearance here tonight prompted me to find out if I've still *'got it'* after all these years. Her reactions to me suggest that maybe I do.

"I'm sure you hear this a lot in your line of work, but you're a beautiful woman," I tell her. Ugh, I sound like an idiot.

"My line of work?" she asks. Her expression turns bashful. "But thanks for the compliment."

"You're a model, aren't you?" I ask.

She waves my question away and giggles. "Oh, I wish."

My heart beats just a little faster. So, she's just another guest here tonight? That means she really doesn't have any obligation to play nice with me or anyone else in attendance. She's standing here, talking to me because she *wants* to.

"You could be, you know." As soon as I've said it, I regret how corny it sounds. But it's the truth. She could have had me fooled.

"You're just being nice." Kayla blushes. "What about you?"

Her question is inevitable, but answering honestly isn't even an option for me right now. I'm not about to flash my wealth in front of her just to score points. I'd much rather see where this chemistry between us goes first, so I feed her an understated answer instead.

"I have a little business of my own," I say. "Retail, as well."

She smiles brightly. "Must be nice to be your own boss."

"Unfortunately, I'm a tough guy to please."

"Oh yeah?" she asks with a twinkle in her eye. "Just how tough are you, Simon?"

That does it. She's taking things further. Why should I play it safe, then?

I scan the shop and note that Lauren is back inside and excitedly chatting to Emily. Everything about her body language has changed. What I'd mistaken for anxiety about the opening turned out to be due to her supposed misunderstanding with Lawrence.

Now that that's resolved, she is reborn. Throughout her talk with Emily, Lauren keeps stealing glances at the new ring on her finger and smiles. How happy she looks now…

Seeing my daughter this way melts my heart and causes my earlier anger to fade. And it soothes my guilt for what I'm about to do.

She's certainly not going to miss me if I step out for a little while. Everything here seems to be under control, anyway.

"If you'd like to drink something other than subpar champagne, perhaps you'd like to accompany me to a nearby bar?" I ask Kayla.

She purses her lips and steals a glance at the group of girls I'd seen her hang out with earlier.

"Just one drink, even. In case you've already made plans with your friends tonight," I add. "I'd like to get to know you better."

She nods and glances downward. God, she's adorable when she's playing coy. "I suppose that would be fine. Just one drink, though."

That was a lot easier than I thought it would be.

I wait by the door while she talks to the tall brunette I saw with Emily before, then picks up her coat. Kayla truly is a sight to behold. If all goes well tonight, I would love to see a whole lot more of her.

"Okay, let's go," Kayla says when she joins me again.

* Kayla *

"You're *not* serious!" Alice says, stealing a glance at Simon over my shoulder.

"We're just going to have one drink. No big deal," I reassure her. "Plus, *you* told me to go talk to him."

She suppresses a smile and shakes her head. "Whatever. Go have fun with what's-his-face. We'll be just fine here without you."

"Simon. His name is Simon," I remind her, and half-turn to look in his direction. God, he's hot. Refusing his invitation, after we hit it off so well, isn't even an option. No matter what Alice says.

"As I said, what's-his-face."

"I'll text you later," I say. Perhaps much, much later. Perhaps after we've already been to bed, rather than just at a bar.

"Behave yourself, okay?" Alice winks at me.

I grin and leave her standing there, while I put on my coat and join Simon by the door. The man is sex on legs. If all goes well, I have zero intention of behaving myself. And the way he's looking at me now suggests we're on the same page.

"Okay, let's go," I tell him.

He nods and opens the door for me. As I walk out ahead of him, I can almost feel his stares on my backside.

This should have bothered me, had he been any other guy. But he doesn't come across as sleazy, probably because we're completely on the same page. I'd made the first move and have been completely in control of our interactions from the start. Now, I'm hoping he will take over and turn things around.

He's a true alpha. Effortless confidence, without even a hint of arrogance showing through. This is a man who goes after what he wants without fear or hesitation. Because nobody has ever tried to oppose him.

Neither will I.

He can have me tonight; he just has to reach out and make it happen. It's all I've been able to think about since I first spotted him.

We make it about half a dozen steps down the road, when his hand finds its way onto my arm. I pause, breathless with anticipation.

"I hope you don't mind." He inhales sharply through his teeth while he looks down at my lips.

Just the tone of his deep voice has me creaming myself. I blink a few times, trying to swallow my nerves as he continues.

"But… I've been wanting to do this ever since you said 'hi'."

My stomach flips and I forget to breathe. His right hand finds my face and his thumb rests against my bottom lip. I lean into his touch, eager for what's to come.

"Me too," I mouth.

I'm helplessly frozen in place as his other hand travels up my arm and across my shoulder until it slips around the back of my neck. He bends just enough to get down to my level and cups my face.

The air between us feels electric when our lips brush past each other for the first time. I hold my breath and wrap both my arms around his broad shoulders. Even through his coat, I can feel the firmness of his body as he presses up against me. Underneath his expensive clothes, he's all muscle.

He kisses me like he owns me already. His mouth, his tongue, his hands mark me as his.

I don't care that we're standing in the middle of the High Street, in that same part of town where I've lived and worked my entire life. It's a small enough place that most people who've lived here a while know each other.

It doesn't seem to matter that my mum might pass us by on her way to the shops. Or one of my neighbours, even an ex-boyfriend or two.

All I have eyes for is him.

Our mouths and hands continue to seek each other out. We're both lost in the moment. Lost in each other.

The chemistry I thought we had while talking, it was nothing compared to what I feel right now. His firm touch on my back makes me feel both empowered as well as weak just for him. Breathless kisses smudge my lipstick against his handsome face. He's oblivious or he simply doesn't care either. What a man. Compared to previous lovers I've kissed, this moment is like day and night.

I was right. Approaching him tonight was either the best or the worst decision of my life so far. I've either hit the jackpot, or I'll wind up broken. Whatever this is, it's a moment I'll never forget for as long as I live.

My first kiss with Simon ends moments later, when he pulls away just enough for me to have a better look at him again. Safe in his arms, time seems to stand still while he gazes at me with those steely grey eyes of his.

"I'm so glad I met you tonight," he says.

My knees are jelly. The words to answer him evade me. All I can think is 'me too', but I force myself to think of a different answer.

"And to think I almost didn't turn up. Lauren's invitation was a little last minute," I respond.

"Lauren has been distracted lately," he says.

"You know her well?" I ask.

"I'd like to think I do; she's my daughter."

"Ah." Well, that's awkward. I don't know her well enough to be sure, but… Assuming Lauren is close to my age, then Simon must be quite a bit older than I thought.

Not that that's a deal breaker necessarily…

Although, the realisation that I have just spent a major part of my brain power imagining sex with a guy about as old as my dad does feel weird to say the least.

"Do you? Know Lauren well, I mean?" Simon's expression has turned thoughtful.

"We're friends," I mumble. *Kind of.* Acquaintances, more like, but I was hoping it would turn into more.

He nods in silence, then slowly releases me from his embrace.

"I want you to know I don't make a habit of flirting with my daughter's friends. Never mind kissing them."

"Yeah, neither do I." I awkwardly shuffle from one foot onto the other and fold my arms. "I don't mind if you don't mind, though."

Maybe I do? I don't know anymore. My tone must reflect my uncertainty, because his demeanour has made a U-turn as well.

Could Simon really be in his fifties? He doesn't look it.

I frown and stare at him to figure it out while he wipes the lipstick off himself. He's stopped looking at me like I'm dessert. A pang of disappointment hits me. I liked things better before we knew this about each other.

Rather than tell him I'm still up for that drink, I decide to take a hint and back away with my self-respect somewhat intact.

"I guess I'd better head back to my friends, then," I say.

He nods. "And I should see if Lauren needs any help."

I press my lips together which so very recently had felt alive underneath his kisses. We could have been good together. In another life.

"No hard feelings," I lie.

"I'm really sorry, Kayla," he says.

Oh God, me too. But I don't say that; instead, I just walk away.

***

"Come on, let's get you home," Alice says while putting her arm around my waist.

I'm upset, and I don't even really know why. So, I kissed a cute guy. It didn't work out. That's hardly the end of the world, and yet…My heart aches more than it should.

I wrap my arm tightly around Alice's shoulders and sigh.

"Why did he have to be her dad, of all people?" I complain loudly. "Couldn't he have just been some random hot older guy. Why can't Lauren have a different dad?"

"I think you had a bit too much to drink, huh?" Alice says.

I shake my head and look at her straight on. My eyes are blurring, so I blink a few times to clear my vision.

"He said I was a model! Can you believe that?" I gesture down at myself. "Me. A model."

"Right. Perhaps I should get us an Uber," Alice mutters.

Why the hell is she talking about me like I'm not even around? I'm right here! I can hear every bloody thing she says, and yet she doesn't seem to realise I'm talking to her.

"Did you hear me? A model!" I repeat. "And I'm fine to walk. It's not far."

Alice finally looks at me. "That might be. But he's still her dad."

"Yeah. He's still her dad." I sigh.

"I mean, how would you feel if you threw a party, invited all of us, and found Amber snogging *your* dad? You wouldn't be happy about it, would ya?" Alice adds.

I pout. "No, I wouldn't be. But then she's a filthy gold digger and even my dad can do better than that."

Alice chucklesnorts. "That's not nice. It was only an example, anyway. What if it was Meg instead?"

"It's true enough, though." I exhale deeply and blink a few times again.

I did have a few too many and my head is totally fuzzy. Tomorrow morning is going to suck in more ways than one.

A fresh surge of unwanted emotions overwhelms me. The last thing I want to do is to get home on my own and start *thinking* about everything. It was hard enough to survive the remainder of Lauren's event with Simon right there across the room. A constant reminder of everything I cannot have.

"Will you stay over, Alice?" I ask. "We could have another drink or two. Or eat a bucket of ice cream, or *something*?" I could really use a friend right now.

She cocks her head to the side. "You know I have to work in the morning."

"Let's just watch a stupid movie, then? Come on!" I whine. "It's not like you're about to cure cancer or something. Live a little!"

"I suppose I could stay for a short while," she agrees.

"Thank you." I sigh and rest my head against her shoulder while we slowly stroll down the street on the way to my flat.

Why the hell did Simon have to be Lauren's dad, of all people? He was the perfect guy otherwise.

CHAPTER THREE

* Simon *

Compartmentalising your emotions is a talent you're forced to learn quickly once you lose a partner. Especially when you have a young child to take care of.

It wasn't easy spending the rest of the evening at Lauren's opening, as though nothing had ever happened with Kayla. Far from it. But I got through it somehow. I managed to swallow my desire for her and focus on the task at hand: being a supportive father to Lauren for her big event.

Lauren has always been my first priority; why should tonight be any different? Stealing Kayla away with the weak excuse of having a drink together was a mistake right from the beginning. I'm going to pay for that one; I already am.

Now that I'm back home, I inevitably find my thoughts returning to Kayla and our little moment outside. In the grand scheme of things, nothing really happened, and yet it changed me.

She changed me.

I pour myself a drink—the single malt I'd been

yearning for all evening—and sit down in my favourite leather armchair.

The amber liquid looks mesmerising in the warm glow of the fireplace. My first sip is too eager. Rather than savouring the flavour of my Scotch, I'm using it to dull my inner conflict.

Tonight has been insane. After everything that happened with Lawrence, and all the anger I felt as a result, I went out and did the exact same thing I hated him for. I went after one of Lauren's peers. Someone else's little girl.

I'd objectified her, lusted after her, and very nearly seduced her too. Because I had no intention of just going out for *one drink,* as I'd told her. One would have turned into two or more. In the back of my mind the end game has always been the same—to conquer her. To take her home and possess her, body and soul.

How could I possibly stoop so low?

I should know better than this!

Kayla's connection to Lauren shouldn't have been a surprise. How many possible reasons could there be for people to attend tonight's event? If she wasn't there for work, it follows that she was there for fun. I thought I knew most of Lauren's friends, and yet I've never heard her mention anyone named Kayla before.

Before I know it, my glass is empty and I'm reaching for a refill. Although I'm feeling the buzz, it does nothing to stop my errant thoughts. As angry as I was at Lawrence earlier, I'm furious with myself now.

It was obvious right from the start that she was significantly younger than me. But when she confessed that they were friends, it really hit home. Guilt overwhelms me along with frustration.

If Emma saw me now, what would she say?

What about Lauren?

If this is a sign of things to come—an impending midlife crisis, perhaps—then I must avoid any future, similar fuck-ups. Troubleshooting is another one of my talents. This time I'll have to troubleshoot not a failing business, but myself.

But not yet. Tonight, I allow myself to *feel* my mistake. Tonight, I mourn.

* Kayla *

I haven't faced Lauren since that night. Today, mere days later, might turn out to be the moment of truth. Alice and the rest of the gang have planned a weekend lunch at a newly opened gastropub nearby, and I'm reluctantly tagging along.

I'm still in a mood when I leave my place and join Alice outside. To make matters worse, the new job I was supposed to join on Monday hasn't materialised. Fired before the very first day.

Cushy office jobs are few and far between for

someone without relevant experience or much of an education. With the economy being what it is, my career prospects are looking bleak.

I'm shit out of luck, and soon will be out of money as well.

"Is Lauren coming, do you know?" I ask her.

Alice shrugs and flips her collar up against the cold. "She said she would."

"Do you think she'll be upset with me? I mean, how was I supposed to know it was her dad?" On the night, she didn't seem bothered. But what if he told her later? What if she saw the way I was looking at him and put two-and-two together? *Ugh*, I hate the uncertainty! On top of that, I'm still feeling sore about how things ended. I miss him, when I never really had him in the first place. Just why I can't seem to put it behind me, I have no idea.

Alice presses her lips together and scrutinises me for a moment. "I would be. But I'm not Lauren. Who the hell knows?"

"I should probably apologise, just in case." I sigh.

Usually I avoid confrontation at all costs. Today could turn out to be spectacularly unpleasant.

"Maybe she doesn't know about what happened." Alice shrugs.

"But if she has any suspicion, it wouldn't be right for me to stay quiet, would it?" I conclude.

"Doesn't know what?" a wind-blown and wide-eyed Megan asks as she joins us at the corner and hooks her arm through mine.

"Nothing," I say.

This is so awkward. A large part of me hopes that Lauren will flake out and I won't have to face her at all. Seeing her will just remind me more of Simon. I don't know if I'm ready for that.

"When are you starting your new job? Monday, right?" Megan asks.

I make a face. "It fell through, so I'm still looking."

"Crap. I'm sorry, yeah?"

I shrug. "So, where's this place you guys picked?"

"It's just near the park," Alice says.

"Maybe I should skip this lunch. I'll be skint soon enough without a job," I grumble.

Alice tugs at my arm to keep me from stopping. "Lunch is on me. Stop worrying so much."

Easy for you to say. You didn't suck face with Lauren's dad earlier this week!

I press my lips together tightly and keep my eyes fixed on the ground as we walk.

When we finally arrive at the place, Lauren is already waiting at the large reserved table in front of the bar. She smiles brightly at us and waves us over.

Oh dear. She has no idea, does she? My heart sinks.

"Hi, nice to see you all again!" Lauren gets up and holds out her arms, and we take turns to greet her.

By then, Alexis and Amber walk in too; we all catch up and then take our seats.

Alice prods me in the side. "Hey, how about applying for a job here?"

I look around. It's been a while since I last did any waitressing. They look fully staffed already, though.

"You're looking for work, Kayla?" Lauren asks.

I nod. "I had something lined up for the new year, but it didn't work out…"

She looks genuinely sympathetic. "That's terrible."

Yep, it is. Not as terrible as the inexplicable ache in my heart, but pretty bad nonetheless.

"Hey, don't you need someone to help out at the shop?" Amber asks from across the table.

Just how and why have I become the main topic of conversation? And it's doubly awkward when I'm hiding such an inconvenient secret.

"No way. I couldn't possibly expect you to do me a favour like that," I stammer.

Lauren pouts. "Emily and I had already hired someone, actually. I'm really sorry."

I breathe a sigh of relief. "You know what they say; don't mix friendship and money." I'm pretty sure they also say *don't make out with your friends' dads*, but I keep that part to myself.

"I know the guy who manages the restaurant at Fulwell Golf Club," Megan chimes in. "I could put in a good word for you."

"It's been quite a while since I've done any waitressing," I say.

"Fulwell is lush. I've been there quite a few times," Amber says. "High class clientele. Tips will be great."

Lauren nods. "It's a really nice place."

"Think about it," Megan says. "My offer stands."

A server appears at our table. "Are we ready to order?" he asks.

Everyone scrambles to look at the menus, which we'd ignored so far.

If I don't find anything on my own, I might just ask Megan for that introduction. If it pays well enough and the hours are flexible, I could still try going back to school like I'd planned.

We've just finished placing our orders when Amber reaches across the table and takes Lauren's hand. The latter looks up in surprise.

"While we wait, do tell me more about *that*." Amber points at the large blue rock on Lauren's ring finger.

Everyone leans forward to get a better look at it. It's beautiful. Expensive, probably.

She blushes and awkwardly pulls her hand away from Amber. "It was a gift."

"That's some gift," Amber comments.

It's not from her dad, is it? I feel the blood rushing into my cheeks. Maybe he felt guilty about what we did too and this is how he's handled it?

"I'm sure whoever gave it to you is something rather special as well," Alice adds.

My stomach twists.

"He is. Very special." Lauren protectively closes her other hand on top of the ring and smiles.

She must be talking about a lover. My relief is short-lived and my earlier melancholy returns. It must be nice to have someone like that in your life. I almost did.

"A man who gives gifts like that is a keeper for sure," Amber comments.

Her comment makes me roll my eyes. Why do we even hang out with her?

It takes a while—and a surprisingly good meal— for the lingering shame and anxiety to fade a little. One thing is certain: I'm not ready to tell Lauren a damn thing about what happened with Simon. Not when I'm still this broken up about it.

* Simon *

Ever since the first of January, I've had an unwanted presence in my subconscious. One which I cannot seem to shake. No matter what I do or how hard I try, she's been there, in the back of my mind, for almost a week now.

I don't dream, really. Or if I do, I hardly ever remember it come morning.

For the first few years after Emma, I'd wake up

certain that she was sleeping beside me. I'd remember whole conversations shared with her at night, which never actually took place. I suppose you could think of those experiences as dreams.

But over time, their frequency reduced, and for the past five or so years, it had stopped entirely. Nothing appeared in its place; it was as though my imagination had died along with her.

However, things changed ever since that single kiss… Even today, early on this first Sunday of the year, I woke up convinced I'd gone to bed with Kayla the night before. Upon closing my eyes, I can still feel her soft skin underneath my touch. The sweet taste of her lips on my tongue. The silkiness of her long blonde hair brushing against my face.

I could swear that remnants of her floral perfume are still clinging to my pillow; to me.

It was so real, so convincing, that before I'm even fully awake, I reach for her side of the bed, only to find it empty and cold.

Of course it's empty. Because none of it ever happened.

I have woken up in my bed alone. Just like every other morning for more years than I care to count.

Rather than get up and go for a run like I usually do, I fold my arms behind my head and stare at the ceiling. It was a beautiful memory, this night with Kayla which never happened. A precious moment in time, which made me feel not like myself, but like someone else with a very different sort of life.

For as long as I fight the urge to fully wake up, I'm not a widower anymore. I'm not a father. I'm just a man, fantasising about a beautiful woman who has caught his eye.

And then the magic fades and guilt and frustration kick in again.

She's Lauren's friend and therefore off limits. She's too young, and the entire situation is unacceptable. To even entertain it goes against every single one of my principles.

I grab my phone and dial Lauren instead. It keeps ringing and ringing until finally switching to voicemail.

I hang up. What am I going to say, anyway? *Hi, please call me because I have no one else to talk to this morning?* Pathetic. I'm supposed to be *her* father, her support. Not the other way around.

She must be either be busy with work, or… I don't dare think too hard about the alternate possibility. Of her, with Lawrence.

That filthy bastard.

Wherever she is, whatever she's doing, she's too busy for her old man. I can't hold it against her. We all have our own lives to live.

And what exactly am I living mine for? It's Sunday, so I don't have any work to distract me with.

What is a man to do when he finds himself frustrated by idle fantasies?

It has been a very long time since Emma passed. Too long.

I'd almost forgotten what it feels like to have an equal to share with. Someone to wake up next to and pull into your arms, just to remind you that the world isn't as cold and empty as it appears to be.

What good is wallowing in self-pity going to do? Nothing.

I have Kayla to thank for making me feel like a man again, not just a dad. Perhaps it's that feeling I crave more than *her?*

What if that's the solution to my current predicament?

I sit up, filled with a glimmer of renewed hope. My troubleshooting skills haven't let me down after all.

It's taken me a painful few days to recover from the setback I faced with Kayla, but now I've got a plan to get myself back to normal. Not to how things were, mind. But back to a *new* normal. I have to re-enter the dating pool. Perhaps I can find what I'm looking for with someone else. Someone appropriate.

Rather than try to call Lauren again, I spend the rest of the morning setting up an online dating profile. It can't be that hard for a successful forty-four-year-old to line up a few dates in this city, can it?

CHAPTER FOUR

* Kayla *

"Hi, my name is Kayla and I'll be your server—" I look up and find Simon's pale grey eyes looking up at me. "But you knew that already," I mumble. God, how awkward is this? It's been a painful three weeks since that ill-advised kiss.

I'm not ready for this.

I'm not over him yet.

"Hi, Kayla," he says. "This certainly is a surprise."

What is it about the way he says my name that makes me feel so weak inside? Goose bumps spread across my entire body. I uncomfortably shift my weight from one leg to the other and fight the urge to scream. How will I survive this?

"Hi. A surprise, indeed." I stare at him a little too long before I catch myself.

What a man. It doesn't help that I already know what an amazing kisser he is. And I've spent many a lonely night wondering what else those lips are capable of. Would he match up to the illicit fantasies I've had ever since our first encounter? Would he exceed them? It hurts to realise that I'll never find out.

The moment we stole didn't even mean anything to him. Why else would he be here, having dinner with another woman? Is she his girlfriend? Was he already with her when we first kissed?

I'd googled him during one of my weaker moments. Half of the front-page results proclaimed him to be one of the top most eligible bachelors of London, with a sprawling real estate business, to boot. But tabloids don't know everything, do they? What the hell was I even thinking?

"Why don't you get us some water, Kelly?" Simon's companion snaps her fingers to attract my attention. "With lemon and a slice of cucumber, okay?"

It grates me that she gets my name wrong, but I don't let it show. I can't let jealousy get the better of me. Not on my first day at the new job.

"Sure. Just a moment," I say, stealing a curious glance in her direction. She's skinny, like an *actual* model. She looks nothing like me. If this is the female company Simon generally keeps, then I'm not sure what he was doing with me that evening.

Men like him don't seriously get involved with losers like me. Not enough pounds in my wallet and too many stuck to my waist. Perhaps he only enjoyed the novelty of it.

I swallow the lump in my throat and leg it back to

the kitchen.

In my rush to get away from Simon and his prickly date, I forgot to hand them their menus. "Shit," I mutter.

"You'll manage?" Gary asks. "If you can't cope, I can take over some of your tables."

I shake my head. "No, no. It's fine. I do need some water with lemon. And cucumber."

Gary points at the bottles in the fridge and then at the bar counter. "Lemon wedges are in that bowl over there; cucumbers, over by the salad station."

"Right. Sorry."

I breathe a sigh of relief once Gary leaves me alone again. Within seconds, I've got my tray with two glasses of water and a lemon wedge and cucumber slice in each. I try to compose myself with a few deep breaths before rushing back to Simon's table.

My hands tremble when I put the two glasses down on the table in front of them. *Remember the bloody menus this time!*

Everything goes wrong when I open one of the binders to the first page and hold it in the woman's direction, inadvertently knocking her glass of water over.

"Watch it!" she snaps.

"Shit, I'm so sorry," I mumble, trying to contain the spill with a napkin. "I'll get you a new glass."

The tablecloth has soaked up most of the water, except for some which has run off right into her lap. She pushes her chair back to inspect the spill, all the while cursing under her breath.

I turn to head back into the kitchen to fetch a fresh glass of water, when she starts berating me loudly.

Fuck. Gary is going to hear.

"I'm really sorry," I plead.

She's having none of it.

"This is dry clean only! You're not supposed to get it wet!" Her eyes are on me like darts and she frantically gestures down at herself.

God, how humiliating! Simon picks up his crisp cotton napkin and holds it in her direction. She's not even paying attention to it, so I take it from him and try to ignore the intense reaction my body has to him when our fingers brush past each other.

"We could dab it off, maybe?" I suggest. "It's only water, after all."

"You're joking, right?" the woman snaps. "This is silk. It's going to leave a water stain!"

My cheeks are red hot with embarrassment as well as anger.

For a split second I want to argue with her. What's the bloody point of clothes if they self-destruct in a little water? And you wore this to *dinner?* Where spills are a real fucking risk? But I don't say any of that, instead I bite my tongue and try to breathe. Wardrobe choices aside, this is still my fault.

"You know what this is? Chanel! Probably costs more than what you make in months!"

My eyes sting and I don't know where to look, so I stare at the floor. "I'm so sorry, honestly. I can get it dry cleaned for you."

"Dry cleaned? It's bloody ruined!"

"It's not so bad, just a splash of water," Simon says. "I'm sure it'll look like new once it dries up. Nothing to get all wound up over."

"Well she should have paid attention to what she was doing! Why is she even working here if she can't manage a simple glass of water?"

"Really! Take my details and let me know about the dry cleaning bill," I stammer.

"No way. This is supposed to be a high-class establishment. At the very least I would expect them to hire experienced staff. I want to speak to your supervisor."

Oh fuck, please don't make me get Gary! He's already less than impressed with me, because I'm a sympathy hire.

I take a deep breath and force myself to speak calmly. "Okay, just a sec—"

Simon raises both hands in a calming motion. "Relax, Kayla. You don't need to call anyone."

"Simon! The clumsy cow ruined my Chanel dress!

There will have to be consequences."

"I didn't do it on purpose!" Despite my best efforts, I've hit my limits and a single tear has escaped the corner of my eye.

"Victoria! That's enough now," Simon barks.

His sudden shift in tone makes me flinch. I steal a glance at the woman—Victoria. She's staring at him with her lips pressed into a fine line.

"But—"

He interrupts her with a shake of his head, then he takes a deep breath. "I will buy you a new dress, alright?"

There's no bloody way the thing is ruined with a couple of sips of water. I want to repeat that I'll take care of the dry cleaning, but there's something about Simon's body language that shuts me right up. For a man as wealthy as Simon, it must seem like we're fighting over scraps.

Victoria glares at me, then turns to Simon again. It looks like she wants to continue ranting at me, but she doesn't. Perhaps she's just had a similar realisation.

"Perhaps you should go home and change," Simon suggests. His voice is ice cold, so different from how he spoke to me earlier. It makes the hairs on the back of my neck stand up.

"But we haven't eaten yet," Victoria says.

A deafening silence follows.

"My driver is waiting outside. He'll take you home," Simon says. "I don't think this was going to work out anyway."

"Fine. I can tell when I'm not wanted." Victoria gets up, glares at the two of us one final time, and stomps out. Was she jealous too? Was that her reason for making this scene?

I'm frozen in place. No idea what I'm supposed to say or do now.

"Everything alright over here?" Gary pipes up beside me. *Of-bloody-course he comes over now.*

"Yes. All fine," Simon says, while picking up one of the menus off the slightly soggy table. "I'll have the steak. Medium rare. And half a bottle of Malbec. The one that isn't on the menu."

Gary stares at me with one eyebrow raised, until I startle into action and note down Simon's order. When Gary leaves us alone a few seconds later, I want to tell Simon I'm sorry.

He'd come here on a date, and my clumsiness ruined it. But I dare not bring it up.

"The steak will be fifteen minutes or so," I mumble.

I reach over and pick up the menus again, when Simon's hand finds my arm. I flinch under his touch.

"Are you okay?" he asks.

The harshness and anger I saw in him moments ago have vanished without a trace. When he looks up at me now, his grey eyes exude a warmth and compassion I hadn't noticed before.

I shrug and make a face. "I'm really sorry. It's my first day. I got nervous."

"When do you get off?" he asks.

My thoughts are jumbled. What is he asking, exactly? Does he mean for me to apologise properly later? Why did he care to ask if I'm okay, then?

"My shift finishes at ten," I say. "Unless I do something else stupid and Gary fires me before that."

His eyes linger on mine and he smiles. "I'll wait for you."

* Simon *

This thing with Victoria was never going to lead anywhere. It was stupid and ill advised, but I'm grateful it happened. Victoria's insistence to have dinner here at Fulwell Golf Club led me right back to Kayla.

Now that I've found her again, I'll be damned if I'm going to let her slip away a second time.

Tonight it taught me two important truths: I can't stand self-important people who treat others like dirt. And, I was wrong to pull away from Kayla in the first place. Worst mistake I ever made.

Because almost every date I'd been on since my supposed epiphany a couple of weeks ago ended the same: in disaster. Every single dinner reminded me why I'd stayed away from the scene all these years. I didn't have the patience to go through the bullshit small talk, when there was no chemistry there.

No woman could measure up to my impossibly high expectations. Except one. My mind wasn't ready to accept it, but my heart knew all along who's right for me.

I find myself sitting here at this table by myself, eating that steak I'd ordered simply to pass the time. And rather than look at my plate, or allow myself to enjoy my overpriced glass of wine, I'm constantly on the lookout for *her*.

Kayla gets off at ten. It's not a long time to wait at all, but I'm impatiently counting the seconds. In truth, I would have waited a lot longer, if necessary.

After Emma, dating had never been a priority for me. At first, I missed her so much that I couldn't conceive of being with any other woman. The years kept on passing and I buried myself in my work, as well as trying to be a good father to Lauren.

But from that first kiss onwards, Kayla had changed me. She awoke something in me that I thought had died along with Emma. It's not the same as it was. This will never replace what I had with Emma, or cheapen the memory of our short marriage.

But together, Kayla and I might share something else, something new.

More than anything, she's making me want to focus on the future, rather than yearn for the past. That's the one promise Emma insisted on during her final days, which I'd broken so far. To look forward. To find happiness once again.

When she stood there, taking all the senseless crap Victoria was dishing out at her, something in me broke. I knew I had started out at the wrong side of this equation. Victoria might have been my date tonight, but I needed to stand with Kayla. Protect Kayla. *Love Kayla.*

Nothing else matters.

She may be too young for me. And I may be a dirty old bastard for even thinking we have a chance in hell together, but I can't help it. During our brief encounter she'd put a spell on me.

When you know, you just know. That was the explanation I'd given to Lauren about Emma and me. She'd thrown it right back at me when I questioned her about Lawrence. And now we've come full circle. Because I've realised now that *that's* how I feel about Kayla.

Kayla is mine. Chance brought us together at Lauren's opening. And it reunited us here today.

Come ten o'clock, I'll confess my feelings to her. Life's too short and fragile not to.

CHAPTER FIVE

*** Kayla ***

Time passes at a snail's pace, but eventually it turns ten, and my shift is over. I don't know whether to be excited or nervous when I approach Simon, who's still sitting at the same table by himself. His eyes are on me already, as they have been for most of the evening. He probably has no idea how vulnerable he makes me feel.

The tablecloth has dried up somewhat, but the evidence of my screw-up is still evident. He doesn't look tense anymore, but that only lessens my embarrassment. It doesn't take it away completely.

"I'm done. My shift is over," I tell him.

"Congratulations," he says, keeping his napkin down and standing up.

"For?"

He's taller than I remember. He makes me feel small and dainty, even though I'm anything but. *A model, me? As if!*

"You survived your first shift without Gary firing you."

I smile briefly. "Right, yeah. It was touch and go

for a bit, but I made it."

He smiles back at me and my heart jumps. He really doesn't look old enough to be Lauren's dad. His closely cropped reddish blonde hair doesn't even have any grey in it that I can see. I would have guessed he's in his late thirties maybe, not even eight years older than me. But I know better now. I'm a lot more informed about him than I was during our first meeting.

"I'd like to talk with you in private, if that's okay?" Simon says.

I find myself helplessly staring at his lips while he speaks. He wants to *talk*, is it? All I want to do is silence him with my mouth.

But that's so very wrong.

I hold my breath and nod. "Sure. I think the function room isn't in use tonight. We could *talk* in there."

He must pick up on my suggestive tone, because he suppresses another smile and gestures at me to lead the way. What am I even doing here? This is a mistake, and yet I can't stop it from happening. I feel like I'm walking head-first into a trap, but I'm unwilling or unable to save myself. Again.

For the past three weeks I've thought about him almost constantly. Initially, I tried to fight it; I tried to forget our kiss. Then, I let my imagination roam free in the hopes that if I kept rehashing things, my fascination with him would eventually fade.

But you don't douse fire with yet more fire.

My misguided efforts of working through my illicit obsession have put me in a position where I find him even harder to resist. Instead of lessening his appeal, it's only made it stronger. How many hours have I spent staring at tabloid photographs of him, fantasising about the impossible?

And I'm leading him into a darkened room at the club to *talk* in private. My imagination conjures up a million possibilities for what's about to happen, and simply talking isn't one of them.

He closes the door behind us and turns to face me. My knees tremble slightly and a shiver creeps down my back.

"Kayla, I owe you an explanation."

Not really, you don't owe me anything. "Okay…"

"Chance put us in an awkward position at Lauren's event."

I nod. "Very awkward." Except, I barely even care anymore now that he's standing in front of me again. I would do it all again, only to regret it later.

"I'm a little rusty at this stuff, so I hope you'll give me the benefit of the doubt," he says.

The look in his eyes just about melts my panties off. It's obvious that he's feeling at least as vulnerable as I am. His demeanour is the complete opposite to how I saw him interact with his date earlier. *Because he cares?* I wonder.

Or maybe he's just that good a player. That's a much more likely explanation, but my heart is unwilling to accept it.

"Okay," I whisper.

The tension between us is almost unbearable. I force myself to keep my hands still, and take a deep breath. It hardly helps; I still feel faint.

"For years it's just been Lauren and I. She was very young when her mother passed away."

My eyes widen as I look up at him. Lauren has never mentioned her parents. When it was just Simon at the opening, I naturally assumed her parents were divorced like mine, and maybe she fell out of touch with her mum.

"I missed Emma like crazy. Never had room in my heart for anyone else—except Lauren, of course."

If he carries on like this, I'm going to tear up. I blink a few times to clear my vision and keep my lips tightly pressed together. As if that'll prevent any unwanted emotions from bubbling up.

"There's no easy way to say this. When I saw you there that evening, something changed for me. *I* changed."

My heart starts racing even faster. Deep down I knew that the kiss we shared that night wasn't meaningless. I couldn't pinpoint why, I just felt it. That's why it hurt so much when our moment passed.

Could it be that he felt it too?

"What are you trying to say?" My voice is still a whisper when I ask my question.

Do I even want to find out if all the assumptions I'm making are true or not? If our kiss meant something to him too, then what was he doing here with that stuck-up woman and her stupidly expensive dress? Surely, I'm just a plaything to him; a toy from a different world.

He takes a deep breath and takes my hand, enclosing it in his. The warmth of his skin burning into mine only fans the fire I've felt for him all along.

"Kayla, I'm not ready to let life pass me by any longer. I need to know if you also felt a spark that night, if there's something here for us to explore?"

I look away from him and try my best to maintain my composure, but my heart is racing and my throat is threatening to close up.

"But, Lauren..." I say. "You're her dad. It's inappropriate. This whole thing is."

He nods and gently squeezes my hand, caressing my knuckles with his thumb. I don't have the courage to pull away; that's how conflicted I am. The heart wants what it wants, but my mind is overflowing with doubts.

"It's not ideal, but that's life for you."

"Like, how old are you, even? How is something like this going to work in ten, twenty years? How is

Lauren going to take it? And you came here tonight on a date with someone else," I mumble. *And I'm a broke loser from a working-class home, whereas you're a multi-millionaire at least.*

I should probably keep my mouth shut if I don't want to scare him off, but I can't. I've been an absolute mess these past few weeks, simply because I have more questions in my mind than I have answers. I know what I *want*, deep down. But there are too many reasons why I should walk away.

He straightens himself and exhales sharply. "Lauren will be fine. She has her own life to live, just as I have mine. This is about what *you and I* want. I only started dating recently because I wanted to *feel* again. It didn't work, until you showed up today."

I glance upwards at him, as though his eyes will tell me everything I need to hear.

"We don't even know each other," I say.

I'm dangerously close to not caring about any of that. Simon is everything I could ever ask for in a man. Why am I still fighting this?

He tilts his head slightly to the side as he looks at me. The warmth in his eyes could make me cry.

I do feel it, too. I feel it in the way my skin reacts to his touch. In the way my chest swells when I catch him looking at me. The way he has infiltrated my entire being, after what—a kiss that lasted barely two minutes? That doesn't just happen. Unless it means something.

"Do you believe in love at first sight?" His voice is raspy when he asks me this final question.

I'm at a loss for words. This conversation isn't easy for him either from the looks of it.

The darkness I recognised in him at Lauren's shop. I know now where it originates.

He's been through so much in life, more than I could even imagine.

What must it feel like to lose someone you love? To watch them waste away in hospital until the very end and then have to explain it all to a little one at home?

I hope I'll never have to find out what that's like.

Am I willing to discount my feelings for him just because he's a little older than me? Because he spent many years as a single father, putting his own love life on the backburner? Filthy rich or not, that's still what he is.

My heart breaks at the thought. No, in this instance, my mind is wrong. It's the heart I have to listen to.

Whatever he wants from me, he can have it all. Damn the consequences.

* Simon *

This is my last stand. Part of me felt it that night at the opening as well. An urgency, like a clicking clock, counting down my chances in life. I'd felt it with Emma all those years ago. We were only kids, but still I was certain that she and I were meant to be.

And then again with Kayla, though I was too ignorant to realise it in time.

What are the chances that I would find that kind of a connection twice? There are people who never get even one such opportunity in love.

It almost seems laughable now that I sought to replace that feeling by going on a bunch of random dates during the weeks since. No wonder I never clicked with any of the women I met. Things never progressed beyond dinner and a few drinks. It wasn't anyone else's fault; it was mine.

So here I am, baring my soul in front of a near-stranger.

And I have no idea how she's going to react. This is what it feels like to jump off a cliff without knowing for sure whether you're heading for water or solid ground.

"Do you believe in love at first sight?" I ask her finally.

She doesn't respond, not at first. And I'm waiting with my heart in my throat, afraid to so much as blink, just in case I miss the slightest hint of where her thoughts are at.

"I never used to," she says after a painful silence. "But I'm starting to change my mind."

I breathe a sigh of relief. "Bloody hell, I thought you were going to ask if I've lost my mind."

The corner of her mouth flutters slightly. "You probably have, to be fair."

I grin. "I won't deny it."

"But I do need some answers," she adds.

If she asks for the world, I'll do my best to give it to her.

"Anything."

Even in the dimmed light of this disused room, she looks radiant. Her cheeks are flush and her eyes are full of wonder. A single lock has escaped the grasp of the tightly coiled bun she's wearing today. I yearn to touch it, but I dare not.

"I want to know your story. About Lauren's mum and you. Tell me everything."

That's all she wants?

I let go of her hand and caress the side of her face with the back of my fingers. Her beauty could make me weep. She continues to stare at me with pleading eyes.

"Sure. Whatever you want to know." I gesture at the row of chairs lining the wall. "It's rather lengthy."

She nods and takes a seat. When I sit down beside her, she rests her hand on my knee and waits for me to start. Her touch distracts, but I will myself to focus.

It's difficult to find the words at first. I've never spoken honestly about those days. In front of Lauren,

I've always put on a brave front.

"We got together in secondary school, Emma and I…" I begin.

Kayla squeezes my knee. My physical reaction to her reminds why I have to do this. She deserves to know.

"She got pregnant with Lauren when we were barely nineteen. It wasn't planned, but we made the best of it. We were so young and naive, but they were good times nonetheless…"

I lose myself in Kayla's gaze and finally, the whole history starts to pour out. When Emma and I married, against her parents' wishes, especially. How I used every penny of our meagre savings to set up my first business when Lauren was barely a month old. How much I loved them both.

By the time I get to those last few months when Emma was in the hospital, tears start to stream down my face. It's probably the first time in twenty years that I've really allowed myself to feel the loss of what once was. I still regret not appreciating it enough when I had it all.

Kayla doesn't say anything, she just keeps on sitting there, listening patiently until I'm done. My heart is raw and wrung out by the end of it.

"Thank you," she whispers.

I nod and force a smile and wipe my eyes with the back of my hand. "This is awkward, huh? I'm not usually this emotional."

She smiles and leans in closer. I can see the shimmer of tears in her eyes too. "It means a lot that you told me. I feel like I know you a bit better now."

I'm still lost in her gaze when I realise that it isn't awkward at all. It's a relief. An unburdening that was a long time coming. Is that why she asked me about it? Because she knew it was necessary?

Neither of us feel the need to speak for the next few minutes. There's so much to see in her. I was correct tonight when I sent Victoria home. It's the first good decision I've made in weeks.

Kayla is nothing like Emma, but I think they might have gotten along. She's not just gorgeous on the outside, she's a beautiful soul. My love for her might be young, but it's uniquely meaningful. I can't let anything stand in our way anymore.

I lean in and close my eyes when her light, flowery perfume hits my senses. This time it's her hands that find my face, pulling me in first for this most awaited second kiss.

Whereas our first short encounter was mostly fuelled by instinct and perhaps lust, I feel something else now. Something deeper, which was always hiding just beneath the surface.

I smile against her lips. If what we have is wrong, I don't want to be right anymore.

Everything I feel, I try to show her, with my lips.

Slow, gentle, and deliberate. Her firm touch on my shoulders gets my heart racing even more.

The passion is still there, even stronger than it was the first time around. But this time it means so much more. During our first encounter I was all ego; my mind was set on conquering her and making her mine. I'd forgotten how good it feels to give up yourself first. To put yourself out there when you have everything to lose.

You might just destroy yourself in the process if you're unlucky. But tonight, I was saved; I jumped and she caught me. I've won the jackpot. If she lets me, I'll spend the rest of my life showing her how grateful I am.

She pulls away from our kiss and smiles at me. The dim light sparkles in her eyes.

"Let's get out of here before Gary locks us in," she says.

I could think of worse ways to spend the night, but I don't protest. We leave the club hand in hand.

CHAPTER SIX

*** Kayla ***

I can't believe what has happened. Today started bleak; my first day at the new job. I was a bundle of nerves and messed up more times than I can count. On top of that, I was fighting that same existential dread which had followed me around ever since my first encounter with Simon.

For weeks I'd felt like I'd lost something which I could never find again.

But it found me. *He* found me.

And he feels it too.

Our first kiss was insignificant, on the surface of it. And yet it really wasn't.

It was profound for both of us and perhaps even more so for him. Our second kiss was so intense it made my memory of the first pale in comparison.

When I first saw him again, part of me wanted to jump him immediately. But now that he's opened up to me, I know we can take it slow. He isn't going anywhere and neither am I.

We head across the parking lot to his car. The driver is already waiting. With his arm around my shoulders, I feel safe. I feel loved.

When I close my eyes, I can sense it so clearly. The warmth in my chest, which tells me everything will be alright now that we're together. We have all the time in the world to see where this leads. Is it all an illusion?

Simon opens the door for me, and I climb in. Soft tan leather, as far as the eye can see. The backseat of Mum's old Renault Clio is a far cry from all this. It shouldn't surprise me, and yet I'm taken aback by the luxury of it all.

"Where would you like to go?" he asks.

Anywhere. I can't say that, can I? *Your place.*

"This is a bit awkward," I say, biting my bottom lip. "But my roommate is quite a gossip. I'd like to avoid her, if possible."

He smiles at me and shakes his head. "Not to worry. Are you hungry?"

I shake my head, even if the opposite is true. "Where do you live?" I ask.

Simon doesn't answer, but instead instructs the driver to take us home. I can't keep my eyes off him; as a result, I have no idea where we're going.

Does it matter? I'll find out soon enough. He means me no harm.

He takes my hand and my heart is aflutter. I want to kiss him again, but it's weird here, with another person in the car.

"You don't care that I'm working as a waitress," I say.

It's not really a question, because the answer is evident in his eyes.

"I care about everything," he responds.

"I always thought I'd go back to school, but I haven't gotten around to it," I say.

"You don't have to justify yourself to me." He smiles.

It would be easy for him to shield himself from all emotion; it's probably second nature after all these years. Still, he isn't distant with me. He's present; as am I. All the confusion I feel, I see the same in him. Tonight, *he* made the first move, when he really didn't have to.

I glance at the driver, who hasn't looked back in my direction even once. Why am I being such a nervous idiot? Wasn't our conversation at the club enough? Why is a part of me still trying to over-analyse everything when he's made it abundantly clear he's all-in already?

"I'm sorry for rambling. I don't know where my head has been these past few weeks."

"Same here." He puts his arm over my shoulder and pulls me closer.

I shut my eyes and rest my head on his shoulder. He puts his other arm around me as well and I find bliss. Surrounded by the herby scent of his cologne, this is my new happy place. It's where I stay until the car pulls to a halt.

We have arrived. The butterflies in my stomach make a reappearance. Who knows what tonight may hold?

Simon gets out first and offers me his hand. Although I'm still wearing my work clothes, he makes me feel like a princess. Cinderella has found her prince. Is there a happily ever after in our future? I'd like to think so.

His house is impressive, as expected. Part of me still can't believe that he really wants me here, in his tastefully decorated living room.

Every time our eyes meet, it strikes me just how content he looks. Gone is the darkness I thought I saw at first.

Simon takes my coat and gestures at me to sit on one of the white leather sofas. He returns after keeping it away and pours me a drink. I have to fight the urge to take over. After spending a whole shift doing just that for others, it's hard to let him serve me.

His crisp white shirt fits him well; a little too well. I can't keep my eyes off his broad shoulders and chest. Soon enough I'll find out what's hidden underneath. My heart speeds up at the prospect.

My fingers linger on his when he hands me the glass. I can hardly breathe. All I want is to take a sip, to deflect. But I don't. I continue to stare into his grey eyes instead. Will I ever tire of this?

Will he? Am I a consolation prize to make up for the love he's lost? The thought crossed my mind before, but I'm not ready to believe it. Lauren and I look very different; I'm pretty sure I look nothing like her mum.

"I'm not really thirsty," I say. Not for a drink, anyway.

"Neither am I."

The corner of his mouth curls slightly and my heart jumps. Those lips. I want what they have to offer.

We put our glasses down on the coffee table without ever looking away from one another. *So, what do you want to do?*

He bridges the gap first; his right hand reaching for my cheek. I love it when he touches me like this. It's so sweet, and yet conjures up images of all the filthy things I want. My eyes snap shut for just a moment and I inhale sharply just to catch my breath. The air is electric again. The tension has grown to dizzying heights.

I'm ready. I want this.

When I open my eyes again, he's still looking at me. I lean in and let my senses overwhelm me. My hand rests on his shoulder, fingers gently tug at the collar of his shirt.

His breaths shorten, as do mine. He reaches for my wrist and coaxes me closer. Our lips fuse again, taking my breath away completely.

I'd mistaken him for a womaniser at first because I didn't know any better. What else was I supposed to think when I saw him there with that horrible woman, Victoria? Although I was hurt, I wanted him anyway. That's just the effect he's had on me from the start.

But now I know the truth. It's been a long time for him. Many years spent without a partner. Although it was a painful story to hear, I don't regret asking him about it. And I'm the chosen one. The luckiest girl alive.

I don't know how and when I end up straddling him, only that I find myself in his lap. His arms keep me firmly in place and he kisses me like our lives depend on it. It's intoxicating, how his tongue dances around mine. How his hands touch me just right to get my blood pumping.

He devours me. I surrender.

I start on his buttons, willing my fingers not to tremble as I open them one by one.

He's gorgeous as expected. The more of him comes into view, the harder I try not to feel inadequate in comparison.

But he gives me little room for doubt. Before I know it, he's made short work of my blouse too. Then he reaches around and pulls out the scrunchie that's been keeping my hair in check. Long locks cascade down and tickle my bare shoulders.

He pulls back for a moment, admiring his handiwork with a smile on his face. I feel like a much desired present, about to be opened for the very first time.

"Perfect," he growls.

My lower abdomen clenches. I'm desperate for things to progress. Underneath me, his body tenses up too. He's hard. He's ready. I can see it in his eyes, feel it in his movements. We're working up to a release that's been three weeks in the making.

I rest my hand flat on his chest for a moment. His heart beats feverishly underneath my touch. Beautifully sculpted muscle, perfect abs. What have I done to deserve all this?

His lips have progressed to my cleavage. My skin lights up underneath his affections. This is what I've dreamed of so many times. He doesn't disappoint.

I hesitate for a moment when I reach the waistband of his trousers, but then I hook my finger in and swiftly undo the buttons.

I kick off my shoes and get up from his lap. He's on his feet in front of me a split second later. His hands make short work of the remainder of my clothes, while I tug his trousers off his hips.

"Bedroom?" he asks.

"Too far."

He grins at me and pushes down his boxer briefs. His erection springs free; my patience runs out. I point back at the sofa. He's letting me be in charge again and I feel powerful like never before.

It doesn't seem to matter that my stomach isn't flat and toned like his. That my thighs are covered in cellulite and stretchmarks. He desires me all the same. Our bodies form a perfect juxtaposition. Masculine and feminine.

Neither of us have much patience for foreplay anymore. His rock-solid length feels about ready to explode when I close my fingers around it. I cast off my panties and straddle him again, slowly lowering myself on top of his thick cock.

"Shit," I hiss.

"You're so tight," he grunts.

Yes. Yes, I am. It's been quite a while for me. Something tells me I'm not going to go without again. Not when he's around.

His hips push upwards into me. His cock stretches my pussy to its limits. Bittersweet pain erupts; I can't get enough of this burn.

I start to ride him; finding my perfect rhythm. He guides me with his hands, but I'm the one setting the pace. Never before have I felt this way. Never has *sex* held so much meaning, so much emotion. I look down into his eyes and find he's already admiring me.

My chest swells with sensations I've never known.

Is this love? In his eyes I see the same question. He probably already knows the answer.

I speed up, riding him harder now. His cock fills me and makes me whole. He covers my chest with kisses, then takes one of my nipples into his mouth and teases it with his tongue. I can't last much longer. My hands twitch involuntarily and my fingernails dig into his upper arm.

His biceps flex and strain under my touch. Red lines appear where I've scratched him before.

By the end of this, we'll both be marked forever. Mentally, as well as physically. And that'll only be the beginning of our story.

My heart aches, but in a good way. I cry out his name, simply because I don't know how else to express myself.

He shifts underneath me and takes over, grabbing my hips even harder and bouncing me up and down. So that's what going to the gym is good for—to be a god between the sheets.

But our limits appear on the horizon. I'm ready to jump across and surrender myself.

"Baby, don't stop," I beg.

Tears sting in the corner of my eyes. *I'm here. I'm yours.*

He grabs a handful of ass and buries his cock deeply into me. My body reacts violently, clenching his whole length, trying to keep it in place.

It's as though my cunt knows it too—he's all ours, and we're never letting him go.

"Oh shit, Kayla!" he grunts.

Like an out of body experience, I stare down at him. His orgasm face is a sight to behold. How his eyebrows pull together, his forehead crunches up into a dozen lines… I'll keep this image with me forever. To relive and cherish this moment: when our first bodily union took place.

His body reacts equally intensely. Muscles contract and release as he deposits his essence into me. I'm grateful to accept it. It's what I've been fantasising about for the past three weeks already and it doesn't disappoint.

My forbidden dream has finally come true.

It's minutes before the fog of ecstasy lifts. And a few minutes more before I catch enough of my breath to speak.

"You're amazing," I whisper. "What did I ever do to deserve all this?"

He runs his hands up my back and pulls me down against his chest. The air feels slightly cold against my damp skin, but his body is still hot. He wraps his arms around me and I let out a contented sigh.

Amazing, how small I feel in his lap, when actually, I'm anything but.

"I know it's too soon. This must all seem very impulsive to you."

I close my eyes and listen to his heartbeat through his chest. One of his hands finds my hair. His caresses are so soothing. I could stay here forever.

"But life's too short to live with doubts and regrets. I meant what I told you at the club earlier. For me, this thing between us, it's love at first sight. I was just too ignorant to recognise it as such."

A little moan escapes my lips. How does he know exactly what to say to slay me? All those reservations I've had about us, they've faded away. I barely remember having them anymore.

"That day, I didn't know what I was feeling either. It was new and completely alien to me. But I know I want to keep feeling it for the rest of my life. With you," I say.

I lift my head and seek out his lips with mine. So beautiful. So addictive.

We share a slow, leisurely kiss. The urgency is over. We don't have anything to prove to each other anymore, because we know the truth already.

He is the one I want; and I'm the one for him.

And to think how nervous he made me only hours before. Ridiculous, when I was the one in control the entire time.

I could tell from the start that he's an alpha; still, he isn't too proud to give up the reins and let me lead. He's lived a whole life before meeting me, but he doesn't lord it over me.

It's a wonderful quality in a man, one which I never knew I needed. I'd certainly never encountered it before. The guys I'd dated before never showed this kind of confidence.

I thought the age gap between us would pose a problem, but it really isn't. It's a benefit.

"You must be tired after your shift," he says. "I hope you'd like to stay?"

Refusing isn't even an option. "Of course, as long as you'll have me."

He chuckles. "Then it's settled."

Simon helps me up, gathers up my clothes, and leads me into the bedroom, where he peels back the duvet for me to get in. It's still odd to have him do these little things for me. But I'm starting to understand that he likes it; this is just another way for him to show that he cares.

The sheets feel cold against my naked skin, but not for long. Simon gets into bed behind me, scoots up really close to my side, and wraps one arm around me to keep me safe. Gone are those nerves from before. Gone without a trace.

In its place, I feel a sense of gratification I've never known. My eyes grow heavier as a result. Today has taken a toll, emotionally as well as physically, and all of it is finally catching up. I nuzzle against his shoulder. He brushes a few errant strands of my hair out of my face and plants a soft peck on my lips.

In this blissful half-dream state, I can't help but think lazily about everything I've learned. About everything he's been through, just to get to this point. About all the doubts I've had, which have been quelled one by one.

There's only one thing I can't yet get past: Lauren. She doesn't know yet; how will she react? He sounded certain that she'll be fine about it, but what if she disapproves?

It's a lot to process, but sleep has caught up. This will have to be dealt with another day, because right now, I'm exactly where I'm meant to be. And deep down in my heart, I'm hopeful that things will work themselves out.

EPILOGUE

*** Simon ***

I wake up in the middle of a beautiful dream.

Kayla and I went to bed together. We loved each other in every possible way, every possible position, until we dozed off. A blonde angel sleeps on the side of the bed that had been empty for much too long. Her perfume hangs in the air, clings to my pillow.

I smile at my mental vision of her. She smiles back at me and closes her eyes again.

I reach for her side of the bed, but find the covers empty and cold.

Still, I continue to smile, because I know it wasn't just a dream. I haven't woken up feeling regret or loss, but the promise of a bright future instead. This is what life was meant to be.

Fate has a funny way of giving you exactly what you need when you least expect it.

As I continue to wake up fully, I think back to how it all happened. How we first met and stole that first kiss out in the street. The confusion that followed, and my utter ignorance about what our encounter meant.

But I found her again and made up for my mistake. She didn't take much convincing, because she'd felt it too. This bond—this connection we shared—neither of us could deny it or resist it.

By the end of our first night together, there was only one doubt left to clear up: How would Lauren take it? I told Kayla not to concern herself with that. I'd handle it, and I did so the very next morning.

Lauren called me a hypocrite, first of all.

Just moments after I'd expressed my displeasure about Lawrence and her at her shop opening, I'd fallen into the very same trap. I'd done what he did and kissed a girl much younger than myself. One of Lauren's peers, someone who should have been out of bounds.

Just one of the little ironies of life.

But after she pointed out all those truths I already knew, Lauren just smiled at me. *I'm sorry, I had to,* she said to me. *I had to torture you a little.*

Actually, my little girl was happy for me; for us. For years she'd been trying to get me to date again, and I never listened. Ever since she'd left home and got her own place, she'd worried about me ending up alone, with nothing but work to keep me company.

I'm supposedly the parent, and she's the child, but in this instance our roles were reversed. Throughout our conversation, I saw a lot of Emma in her. How she always used to look out for others first, rather than herself.

Kayla and I had Lauren's blessing. We had nothing to worry about anymore.

And the rest, as they say, is history.

I open my eyes again to the sound of the shower in the en-suite. That's enough to force me out of bed.

By the time I reach the bathroom, the large glass cabin is starting to get steamed up already. I can just about see Kayla's silhouette through the fog.

"Mind if I join you?" I ask.

She turns and smiles at me when I enter. She's even more beautiful like this; no makeup, wet locks sticking to her face. This is the face no one else gets to see.

"Morning," she says.

I put my arms around her and respond with a kiss. I love how her curves press up against me. My body is hard and lean; hers is feminine and luxurious. We complement each other perfectly.

Her fingers dig into my back, encouraging me to go a little rougher on her.

"You're insatiable, aren't you? After everything we did last night?" she teases.

I smile into her lips and continue to taste her. Sweet perfection. Everything we did, I could do it all over again right now.

Her hand travels downwards and finds my cock already hard just for her. During the short time we've been together, we've done it countless times, in countless ways, yet it never gets old. I'm a horny teenager all over again, just for her.

"Just catching up on lost time," I say while guiding her backwards and pinning her to the wall.

"Wow, those tiles are cold!" she yelps. Yet she makes no efforts to stop me or move away.

"Allow me to warm you up then," I counter.

She hitches her leg up, allowing me access to her exquisite pussy. I circle her clit with my finger, then slip it inside. She readily accepts me and grinds her hips against my hand.

Beautiful.

Seeing how she reacts gives me purpose. Her pleasure is my command. I know what she wants; it's the same thing I crave too.

Her hands seek out my body. She knows it's all hers. Just as her body belongs to me now.

The tip of my cock brushes past her thigh. It's enough to make me lose my patience and my sanity. She angles her hips just so, eager for everything I've got to give. There's a time and place for foreplay, but right now isn't it.

I guide it in with my hand. As soon as I've entered her depths, instinct takes over completely. I am possessed.

They say it's uncomfortable, having sex in the shower. I've not found that to be the case. It's more difficult to resist it, when I know I have all this to look forward to.

I reach for her thigh and keep it steady around my hip. The wall at the back keeps her in place for all I'm about to unleash.

Again, and again, I thrust into her. Every time I do, it feels just a little more intense. One step closer to salvation.

She started with soft nibbles on my neck, but soon she starts using more teeth. With one hand on my arse, she lets me know just how fast she wants me to go. This morning, she wants it rough and quick.

I love when her affections grow firmer and clumsier, signalling her growing pleasure. She's getting there. It won't be long now.

Kayla is everything I am not. Caring, beautiful, gentle, and kind. It's my job to keep her safe, to make her happy. I'll spend the rest of my life doing just that. And the best way I know how to is like this.

Buried deep within her, I become worthy. In her embrace, I am at home.

Her breaths quicken, her touch turns erratic. Her release is within reach, and I know exactly how to get her there.

My hand seeks out her ample breast. Soft, luscious perfection, just like the rest of her. My goddess; my love. I run my thumb across her hard nipple, and she melts against my touch.

"Don't stop," she cries out.

I don't intend to. My movements speed up. My own orgasm starts to creep up on me, but I force myself to focus on hers instead. *Ladies first.*

Harder. Deeper. Faster.

Her face tenses up and she calls out my name. Fingernails dig deeply into my shoulder blade, giving me that sweet ache I have come to crave so much. Her pussy clenches down hard on my dick and I lose control. Now that she's done, I'm free to join her in my own release.

My balls contract, and hot seed gushes into her. I shudder to a halt deep inside, unwilling for this moment to end.

We're both still gasping for air. Despite the constant stream of water raining down on us, I can feel fresh sweat appear on my skin. A reward for my efforts, better than any workout or morning jog, and infinitely more satisfying.

We've done this so many times, and yet I find myself marvelling at her gorgeous post-orgasmic face. Her expression slowly calms; her eyes open and she blinks at me through wet lashes. I've made this happen. I've pleasured her and she's made me whole.

She smiles at me. "I wish we could just spend the rest of the day in bed."

"Same here." I run my hand through her wet hair and lean down for one last slow kiss.

We both know we can't, though. I have a business to run and she has to get to class, and then to work later. Ever since she's gone back to college, our schedules have become quite hectic and full. But absence makes the heart grow fonder. We cherish every moment we get together until we are forced apart again.

Tonight, we'll celebrate our reunion a little differently. I intend to make it a night to remember.

"I'll think about you all day," she says.

Same here, more than you know. I smile back at her. "I love you."

"Love you too."

I watch as she rinses herself off one final time, then steps out of the cabin and grabs her towel, leaving me alone with my thoughts.

Although I do have to get to the office this morning as well, I've cleared a few hours from my schedule without telling her. After lunch, I'll go jewellery shopping with a clear mission in mind.

This thing we have together is wonderful, but it's not enough for me. I'm old-fashioned that way.

By the time she gets home, I'll have a surprise waiting for her. A symbol to formalise our love, accompanied by the most important question a man could ever ask.

By tonight, I hope she'll accept my proposal and we'll go to bed not as boyfriend and girlfriend, but as something a lot more.

Before the sun goes down, I hope she'll agree to be my wife.

AUTHOR'S NOTE

Thanks so much for reading *Coffee & Curves, Books 0-2!*

Perhaps you've been following me for a while, perhaps you're new to my work. But now that you're here, I'd like to give you a little background on how this book came to be...

My writing career started all the way back in October 2012 when I took a very deep breath, closed my eyes, crossed my fingers and even my toes and clicked 'Publish' on my first short story. That steamy little piece called *Ladies' Day,* and the book it grew into eventually (Beautiful Stranger) are still relevant today because it features a curvy heroine and her more mature lover. It serves as my first foray into steamy body positive romance.

Since then, I've published a whole bunch of books, in various romance sub genres; as L. Moone I write contemporary, and as Lorelei Moone I write about shifters, vampires and other paranormals. Certain themes tend to repeat themselves throughout my catalogue.

Beauty lies in the eye of the beholder. The hang-ups we tend to have about ourselves and our bodies usually aren't shared by the opposite sex. While it's a lot more popular to write about gorgeous curvy ladies and their athletic admirers than the other way around, I've covered both. More often than not, you'll find a larger man paired up with a petite woman in my catalogue as well (Husky Men Do It Better series).

Love at first sight is another theme I write about quite a lot, both in my paranormal books as well as the contemporary ones. In fact, I have an entire series called Chance Encounters that follows three couples who casually hook up, only to find that they don't really want to say goodbye after. What they recognized as lust, turned out to be something a lot more intimate.

If I had to pick a third, then it would be messed up characters. Perfection is boring to me because if you put two flawless people together there's no conflict; no drama! Some of my characters have physical flaws, while others might be a bit neurotic or otherwise eccentric. That's what keeps things interesting for me as a writer.

Anyway, this bundle contains the first three titles in my ongoing Coffee & Curves series of contemporary Instalove Romances. These shorter books are a bit of a guilty pleasure for me as a reader, so it's but natural that I wanted to have a go at writing them as well. I hope you enjoyed the first three, and will follow along to read the remaining books as they come out.

And that's enough from me. I hope you enjoyed the story as much as I did while writing it, and if you're interested in reading more of my work, perhaps you'll consider signing up for my newsletter. I'll even give you a free short story when you sign up.

x, Lorelei

FIND ME AT:

- ❖ LMoone.com
- ❖ Lorelei Moone on Facebook
- ❖ AuthorLMoone on Instagram

I also write Paranormal Romance as Lorelei Moone. Check out LoreleiMoone.com for more information.

L. MOONE

www.ingramcontent.com/pod-product-compliance
Lightning Source LLC
Chambersburg PA
CBHW070630170726
48291CB00003B/961